Kind of a Bad Idea

A BAD DOG ROMANCE

THE MCGUIRE BROTHERS
BOOK SEVEN

LILI VALENTE

Kind of a Bad Idea

The McGuire Brothers
A Bad Dog Novel

By Lili Valente

Created with Vellum

About the Book

Seven Trevino is a "bad boy" single dad with a heart of gold and a body a Viking king would kill for.

He's also my best friend. A friend I wish could be more, but he refuses to even *consider* dating.

He's convinced he's too old for me.

But I know he feels the electricity that crackles in the air every time we touch, and I don't care about our age gap.

All I care about is that no one has ever made me feel as safe, understood, or desperate to get naked as Seven does.

So when we end up stranded in the woods together after his daughter pulls a Parent-Trap scheme for the ages, I'm in no hurry to find a way back to civilization.

I intend to take advantage of every second of being trapped in a tiny cabin with this man.

Every moment of sharing that one bed...

Every moment of feeding the fire building between us...

And turns out, Seven feels the same way.

Soon we're christening every surface in the cabin--and the outdoor tub on the porch--and I'm positive my dreams are coming true.

But can our fledgling relationship survive in the real world? Or will Seven's determination to "protect" me shatter both our hearts?

For all the misfits. I love you.

Chapter One

Beatrice "Binx" McGuire

A stubborn burrito of a woman stuffed with recalcitrant beans and topped with obstinate sauce...

I'm insane.

Truly, out of my mind.

That's the only explanation for why I continue to do this to myself, though Seven has made it abundantly clear that he only wants to be friends.

Friends, that's it.

Not even friends with benefits or kissing friends or friends who hold hands when they've had too many martinis at his mother's dive bar. I can't even get a longing look across the bank lobby when he comes in to make a deposit.

And yet, here I am, lingering at the entrance to my brother's wedding reception in a clingy gold sweater that shows a hint of my black bra underneath, crossing all my fingers that the bearded bad boy of my dreams is about to stride up the hill from the parking area.

"It's getting late," Wendy Ann, my little sister says, stretching out on the lounge chair she dragged to the end of the vineyard's driveway. She has a blanket over her legs, but the night is surprisingly warm for mid-October, the perfect evening for dancing the night away with the people we love. "I'll make sure no uninvited guests crash the fun. Go enjoy the party. I've got this."

"Nah, I'm good. I'll keep you company a little longer." I glance over my shoulder at the brightly illuminated tent crouched beside the vines. The band just launched into a cover of The Way You Look Tonight, and half of the guests are still in line at the buffet. "They haven't gotten to the fast songs yet."

"So?" Wendy Ann asks. "It's still dancing. You love dancing. I, however, understand that dancing is a gateway drug."

I arch a brow her way. "To what? Enjoying yourself?"

"To losing focus." She sniffs and pushes her glasses higher on her nose, though there isn't much to see out here at this point. The sun set an hour ago, and only the faintest pink light lingers on the horizon, making the surface of the lake glow in the distance. Soon, we won't be able to see anything beyond the gas lamps flickering along the drive leading down to the parking lot. "And I refuse to lose focus. I have four fellowships to apply for tomorrow."

I hum beneath my breath, willing the sound of a motorcycle engine to cut through the air. It's Saturday night, Seven's one night off kiddo duty, and it's not like there's a lot to do in Bad Dog. Surely, he didn't get a better offer than a McGuire family wedding reception. Yes, the reception is taking place a full month after the bride and groom eloped to Las Vegas, but it's still going to be a banger.

Say what you will about my family, but we know how to party.

Except for Wendy Ann, my nerdy baby sister, who I'm beginning to think is allergic to fun.

"Oh, come on, you can take one day off," I say. "Tomorrow is Sunday, the Lord's Day. And the Lord wants you to stay in bed nursing a hangover and eating nachos. That's why he invented Sundays."

She rolls her eyes. "Easy for you to say. You're not living with Mom and Dad. There's no sleeping in at that house. Dad's up by five a.m. slamming cabinets while he makes coffee, and Mom hits the exercise room at five-thirty to blast Jane Fonda."

My upper lip curls. "That woman is permanently stuck in the 80s. Does she still wear hot pink leggings and the leotards with the string up the butt?"

Wendy Ann shudders. "Yes, and Dad still follows her around like a horny puppy after, patting her sweaty bottom while she makes breakfast." She sticks out her tongue with a soft gagging sound. "It's so disturbing. I have to land a position and move out before Thanksgiving, or I'll lose what's left of my will to live."

"Valid," I say. "Though, you know, you could always crash on my couch, if you wanted. I'm pretty sure Drew has a spare room he hasn't filled with kids yet, too. He'd probably let you stay for free if you helped out with babysitting every once and a while."

Wendy Ann sighs. "Thanks, but that would hurt Mom's feelings, and you know how she is."

"A living nightmare?" I mutter beneath my breath, not wanting to think about my mother right now.

At the last family wedding, she tried to convince my father to physically subdue me so that she could cover my tattoo with makeup. And she still hasn't quit giving me shit about shaving my head last January, even though it's grown out to my chin, and is cut in a shaggy bob that's pretty cute, if I do say so myself.

I never told her the real reason I shaved my head—that I was helping raise money for Seven's daughter's cochlear implant surgery. Even my image-obsessed mother would have been proud of me for helping a deaf girl hear music again, but I didn't want her understanding because I'd done a good deed. I wanted her to accept that my body is *mine* and whatever I do with it—tattoos or haircuts or showing a hint of bra under my sweater—is my right.

And it doesn't mean I'm a bad daughter or unworthy of love.

Wendy Ann sighs again. "She's not a nightmare. She's just Mom. I'm sorry you're on the black sheep list this year, though. Seems like we all get a turn on it, sooner or later."

"Not you." I nudge her sensible black pump with the toe of my shiny leather boot. "You're the brilliant baby of the family who can do no wrong. Mom hasn't stopped talking about you graduating with a 4.2 since May."

Wendy Ann slaps a hand to her face. "I know, God, I'm sorry. It's so embarrassing."

"Yeah, well, stop being so smart and awesome then, okay? You're making the rest of us look bad."

"No, you're making yourself look bad, at least to Mom," she says, peering at me over her fingers. "Did you really have to quit your job *now*? When you're already on the naughty list? You realize Mom is going to give birth to a litter of kittens when she finds out you left the bank."

I roll my shoulders and stretch my neck to one side. Just thinking about the inevitable fallout is enough to make my muscles coil into knots. "She knows I've been apprenticing with a tattoo artist."

"Apprenticing a couple nights a week as a hobby is very different than quitting your stable job with health benefits to scar people for life full time."

I snort as I pace away from her chair. "They're not scars. They're decorations. Symbols of empowerment! Memories and mission statements and happiness written forever on the skin so you never forget the best parts of your life." I spin, fisting a hand in the air as I pace back the way I came. "They're art. And they're my passion. This is why I quit the bank, Wendy Ann. I've already wasted too much time in a job I hate. It's time to follow my bliss."

"Yes, I understand, and *I'm* happy for you," Wendy Ann says. "But that's not how Mom will see things, and you know it."

I blow out a breath, deflating as I wheeze, "Yeah, I know."

"Just be sure to have your ducks in a row before she finds out. You'll need to show proof of ongoing health insurance. I would also suggest a financial prospectus for your net income after expenses for the next five years, as well as the balance statement for your 401(k). I can help you put a spreadsheet together if you want. She loves a spreadsheet."

"Right," I say, not bothering to tell Wendy Ann that I stopped contributing to my 401(k) two months after I started at the bank as a junior loan officer. I just wasn't making that much money after taxes, and I've never been the type to put off fun today for safety tomorrow.

Nope, I'm a "live in the moment, grab fun by the balls, and worry about what happens when the balls turn out to be sweaty and gross and infect you with a strange fungus later" kind of girl.

Which is why I sent Seven that invitation, even though he's never officially met my family and doesn't always play well with others. I thought we'd have fun together. I planned this party, after all. That means the band is top-notch, the booze is flowing freely, and there are plenty of fun things to do when you're tired of drinking and dancing. I have lawn bowling set up behind the vineyard tasting room, a photo booth with dozens of props, a candy buffet, frisbee golf, and a few punching bags dangling from the trees not far from the tent.

The punching bags are mostly for me, in the event I need to blow off steam after another run-in with my mother.

She's already told me to go put on "a real shirt," hissing something about protecting the eyes of innocent children as I hurried down the hill to join Wendy Ann at the check-in spot. But I ignored her, of course. My bra is modest and covers way more of my breasts than my bikini top, which every child here has seen at the annual McGuire family lake party. It's fucking ridiculous, especially considering my teenage cousins are wearing dresses so short. I saw Kayley's entire ass when she leaned over to grab a handful of gummy worms across the candy table.

I was grateful for the excuse to hide from the party for a while, manning the check-in table and informing people looking for dinner at the winery that it's closed for a private party.

But now, the check-in table is bare, save for two goody bags—one for my brother, Barrett, who is at the hospital delivering a baby with bad timing, and one for Seven, who is making it clear, once again, that we are just friends. We will not be swaying to a slow song or flirting over a heated bout of lawn bowling or stealing a kiss in the photo booth. I am still "too young for him," despite the fact that I'll be turning twenty-seven in two weeks.

My parents had three children by my age, and I'm not the least bit worried about dating a guy in his early forties or becoming a stepmom if things get serious between us. I adore Sprout, Seven's eight-year-old daughter, and she feels the same way about me.

Hell, if it weren't her night to hang out with her grandma, I would have invited *her* to the party.

Sprout knows how to have a good time, and watching her dance to music she can finally hear—instead of just feeling the beat in her body—is magical. Sometimes, I'll look over at her, wiggling to whatever she put on the jukebox at her grandma's bar, and get choked up watching her spin in giddy circles. She loves music so much, the same way I loved art as a kid. It speaks to her sweet, sassy soul, and I'm so thrilled to have played even a small part in making her surgery possible.

I would shave my head every month for the rest of my life to watch that kid shimmy to Me and Julio Down by the Schoolyard, no matter what my parents had to say about it.

And I would gladly skip having biological children for a chance at forever with Seven.

He's made it clear he doesn't want any more kids. It's one of the ways he tries to scare me away, by sharing the news that he's had a vasectomy with alarming frequency whenever I happen to be present.

But I'm not scared. Hearing he's shooting blanks just makes me excited about all the fucking without condoms we could do if he'd just open his eyes and see how perfect we'd be together. We both love tattoos, hitting the gym, and riding motorcycles. We share a passion for the outdoors and spontaneous adventures, and I make him laugh more than anyone in the world, even Sprout.

Seeing Seven's ruggedly handsome, occasionally menacing-looking face split into a big grin that *I* put on his lips is one of my favorite things in the world. He goes from dangerously handsome to wickedly cute in the blink of an eye, and his laugh warms me to the marrow of my bones.

It also turns me on.

Every time he laughs, my nipples get hard, which is part of the reason I ripped the padding out of this bra.

In the event that he showed up tonight, I wanted him to see what he does to me. I have reached the "shameless showcasing of nipples" stage of my crush on this man, which is probably a sign that I should step back and take a hard look at my life choices.

Do I really want to spend another year lusting after a guy who calls me "kid" and ruffles my hair like I'm his little sister? Do I want to spend another night at his place, grilling burgers and playing board games while falling even harder for Seven and Sprout, only to be tucked into the guest room alone when I'm too tired to drive home?

Do I really want to run into him in town on another one of his blind dates? Those blind dates that have gone nowhere so far, but will inevitably lead to Seven finding a girlfriend and having less time to spend with his "buddies," of which I am considered one?

A buddy.

Blargh! I don't want to be his buddy. I want to be his sex goddess, the object of his fascination, his heart's desire. I want him to lie awake thinking of me the way I lie awake thinking of him, or at least be unable to resist an invitation to come party with me.

So maybe...

Maybe I should go dance with one of the few single men I'm not related to and consider expanding my horizons. Maybe I've finally met a human even more committed to stubbornly sticking to his guns than I am.

I'm about to tell Wendy Ann that we should both head up to the tent and have some fun—let any would-be diners crash the party if they want—when I hear it...the rumble of a motorcycle.

Heart leaping into my throat, my nervous system lights up like Times Square on New Year's Eve. The hairs lift at the back of my neck, my lips start to buzz, and suddenly, it's all I can do not to break into a victory dance in the middle of the drive.

Because I would know that softly-purring engine anywhere.

That's Seven's vintage, two-tone Chief, the one I helped him rebuild last summer, while obsessing about how sexy he looked with sweat running down into the neck of his white cotton t-shirt as we toiled in his garage.

He's here! He came!

We're about to spend our first Sprout-free evening together since the night we guarded her chickens from a particularly determined fox in his backyard last spring. Since the night he ran his fingers over my face, told me I was beautiful, and came so close to kissing me that I would have sworn he felt the potential simmering between us, too.

The sexual tinder waiting for a spark to set it ablaze...

"Woah, who's that?" Wendy Ann asks, sitting up in her lounger as Seven rumbles up the drive, bypassing the parking area and heading straight for us.

"That's Seven."

"Holy sexy beast and a half," she mutters, popping to

her feet beside me. "No wonder you have a crush. He's outlandishly good-looking."

"Outlandishly," I agree.

"His hair is like a luxurious pony mane," she breathes. "And I think his thighs are as big as my entire body."

"He has amazing thighs," I murmur, fighting a goofy grin as he draws closer. Discreetly, I flap a hand at Wendy Ann. "Now scram."

"No way, I want to meet him," she says, pushing her glasses up her nose. "You never let me meet your boyfriends."

"Yes, I do," I counter, raising my voice to be heard over the approaching engine.

"No, you don't. You always made me go upstairs to my room before your boyfriends picked you up."

"That was in high school, when you were an annoying middle school goober. And he's not my boyfriend," I say, with a soft swat on her thigh. "But fine. Just play it cool, okay?"

But I don't get the chance to see if my sister is capable of playing it cool. The moment Seven swings off his bike —before I can begin the introductions—he jogs toward us with a frantic look in his dark eyes, demanding, "Is she here?"

I blink. "What? Is who here?"

"Sprout," he says, running a hand over his head, smoothing the hair that's escaped from his ponytail away from his face. "Mom went upstairs to take a shower. When she came back down, Sprout was gone."

My fingers fly to my throat as panic dumps into my

bloodstream. "Oh my God. Was there any sign of a break-in or—"

"No," he says, shaking his head. "And Mom said she was complaining about missing the party before she went upstairs. Sprout saw the reception invitation you sent and has been begging me to take her all week."

"You should have told me. You could have both come. But no, I haven't seen her." I turn to Wendy Ann. "What about you? Did you see a little girl with long, wavy brown hair the same color as Seven's sneak in at some point before I got down here? Or maybe while I was helping Aunt Cindy up the hill?"

"She would have been wearing a green dress," Seven adds, his voice vibrating with worry as he shifts his focus to Wendy Ann for the first time.

Wendy Ann bites her bottom lip, shaking her head. "No, I don't think—"

"Green and white stripes," Seven cuts in. He motions around his waist, holding his hands out a good foot from his hips. "With a fluffy, scratchy thing underneath that makes it stick out. My mom said it was missing from her closet."

My sister's forehead smooths as her brows shoot toward her hairline. "Oh, yes, maybe! There *was* a little girl in a fluffy dress like that with the Simons. I assumed she was their granddaughter or something, but maybe not. They should still be up there. No one's left yet." She motions toward the tent, but Seven is already on the move.

"Thank you," I tell Wendy Ann, turning to run after him.

"I'll come help!" she calls from behind me, but I don't slow my pace.

Wendy Ann has spent the past six years hitting the books, not the gym. There's no way she'll be able to keep up with Seven. I'm having a hard time myself, and I added extra sprints to my cardio regime last month in advance of an obstacle course race I want to do in the spring.

But that's what terror does to a person—it delivers one hell of an adrenaline rush—and Seven is clearly terrified. I've never seen him this worried. He's usually the coolest cucumber in the room, the kind of man who can stop a bar fight in its tracks with one hard look and a raised brow.

But this is his baby, his world.

His devotion to his daughter is one of the many things I love about him.

Realizing I dropped the "L" word again in my mind, I run faster, determined to be by his side when he finds Sprout.

Chapter 2

Seven Trevino

A man about to yell at his daughter.
Then hug his daughter.
Then yell at his daughter again.
Then hug his daughter again.
Then tell his daughter that she's grounded for the
next ten years, and that if she keeps
trying to Parent Trap him into
dating Binx McGuire, she can consider that
grounding effective until she's thirty-five,
or a nuclear physicist, whichever comes first.

S he's here. She's probably on the dance floor.

Or by the dessert station, sneaking cake.

Or watching the band play and drumming along on whatever hard surface she's found nearby.

Binx's sister said that she saw her.

Thought *that she saw her... She could have been wrong. Sprout could be walking down a highway in the dark right now, about to be kidnapped, and it's all your fault*, the terrified voice in my head pipes up, making me run faster. My lungs burn as I crest the hill and aim myself for the large tent beside the tasting room.

She has to be here.

She just has to be.

And when I find her, she's so grounded, so fucking grounded. She thought our lives were boring before? She has no idea how boring I can make things for her.

Hell, I'll move us out to my land outside of town and homeschool her in the wilderness if that's what it takes to keep her safe. Her only friends will be the squirrels, the rabbits, and Tater Tot the groundhog, who lives in a burrow under the old shed.

I *should* move out there. The main lodge and new outbuildings are ready to go, but I could use the extra time to work on renovating the cabin we'll use as our home when I'm running the retreat next summer. And without a soul around to set me up with, Sprout will have to give up on this crazy fantasy of hers, the one where I'm in love with Binx McGuire, and all I need is a push from my sweetly meddling kid to live happily ever after with the woman of my dreams. (And the stepmother of hers.)

But I'm not in love with Binx.

I'm obsessed with Binx. I think about Binx at least twenty times a day and dream about her every night. I've drawn fifteen different versions of her mouth in my sketch pad, call her way too often, and keeping my hands off her is basically my third full-time job.

Even tonight, with fear for my daughter burning through my blood and terror clutching at my throat, a part of me still sat up and took notice of "my bestie's" see-through sweater and the black bra beneath.

That kind of attraction is fucked up. Dangerous. I learned that lesson the hard way. And while I can't pretend to be the poster child for good decisions, I never make the same dumb mistake twice.

I will never lay a hand on Binx. I will never be anything but her friend, no matter how good she smells or how sexy she looks dancing by the jukebox at my mother's bar or how many times her eyes light up when she looks at my baby girl.

I love Sprout too much to ruin that relationship for her.

I *would* ruin it, there's no doubt in my mind. That's what I do when I fall like this. I hold on too tight, cling too hard, dive too deep. I scare people away, even good people. Even the best ones, like Binx.

She's right behind me. I can hear her footsteps hitting the ground. She's probably as scared as I am. I feel bad about that, and about barreling up to her family's party like a rampaging barbarian, but not bad enough to waste my breath speaking to the older woman who asks, "Can I help you?" in a passive-aggressive voice as I push past her, moving swiftly toward the dance floor.

I have one mission, one focus, one—

"Oh, thank God," I mutter, my shoulders sagging as my stomach turns itself inside out.

She's there, at the far corner of the dance floor, bouncing around with several other kids to the band's cover of Do You Believe in Magic. My daughter, my reason for living, is safe.

And now I'm going to make her wish that she was never born.

Or at least that she never thought about leaving the house without permission and will *never* do so again.

"Wait," Binx pants, grabbing my elbow and holding on tight. "Don't make a scene. You'll embarrass her."

"Good," I say, glowering down into Binx's bright blue eyes. She's rimmed them with eyeliner and some kind of sparkly eyeshadow that makes them even more striking than usual.

She's fucking gorgeous tonight. But then, I knew she would be. Even in sweatpants and one of my ratty old t-shirts hanging to her knees, she's beautiful. Dress her up for a wedding reception and she's irresistible. That's why I didn't come. I know better than to put myself in situations that test my resolve.

"No, not good, you don't want to do this," she says, tightening her grip on my arm. Even the feel of her fingers pressing against my skin through my sweatshirt is enough to make me ache to wrap her legs around my waist and take her against the nearest tent pole.

Something I'm sure her family would *love*.

They're already staring and whispering. Some speculate about who the angry man in jeans and the tattered Tool sweatshirt is. Others hiss all the details of my dive-bar-owning mother, garbage father, and time spent in prison into their friends' ears as quickly as they can vomit up the hot gossip.

It's been over twenty years since I was that stupid, messed up kid who got into trouble with his friends and ended up paying the price—and I didn't even live in Bad Dog at the time—but to most people in this town, I will never be anything but a piece-of-shit ex-con. They wouldn't want their daughters sitting next to me at the diner, let alone dating me.

Binx hasn't even told her parents that we're friends, but I can't blame her. Her mother has a pole stuck up her ass, and from what I've seen at the hardware store when I stop in for renovation supplies, her father isn't much better.

That's another reason I ignored her invitation. I didn't want to get her into an uncomfortable spot with her parents.

But looks like it's too late for that now...

Everyone is staring, and I mean *everyone*. I'm sure her mother and father are getting an eyeful, and that Binx is going to get an earful later.

It's that, as much as Binx's gentle insistence that we talk before I push through the crowd to snatch Sprout up in my arms, that convinces me to follow her out of the tent. We step into the shadows outside the brightly lit gathering, but Binx keeps going until we reach what looks like a mini carnival.

There are games set up in the grass beneath softly glowing solar lamps, a photo booth, and what looks like...

"Are those punching bags?" I ask, already headed that way.

"Yeah. They're for my mother," Binx says, falling in beside me. I shoot her a confused look and she adds, "Not for her to punch. For *me* to punch, when she drives me crazy." She stops beside the closest bag, holding it lightly on either side. "Listen, I know you're angry, and you have every right to be. What Sprout did was wild and dangerous and wrong, and she deserves whatever punishment you, as her father, decide is best."

"I know," I say, my hands curling into fists.

"But you also know that she's had a hell of a time making friends," she adds in a softer voice, clearly mindful of the older kids playing frisbee golf not far away. "And she's so happy right now. She's having a great time dancing with kids her own age for the first time ever. I don't know about you, but I feel like there's a way to honor that, to let her have a little win, while also holding her accountable for her actions."

I shake my head. "She snuck out of the house at nine o'clock at night."

"I know."

I jab an arm toward the entrance to the vineyard. "And somehow made it five miles down the road in the less than twenty minutes that Mom was upstairs in the shower. That means she didn't walk."

Binx nods, her brow furrowing. "I know. And the thought of her hitchhiking her little ass up here terrifies me, too. Truly. Really, really bad things could have happened, but...they didn't. Which means you have the chance to teach her this lesson in a kinder, gentler way than a kidnapper would have."

I shudder and press a fist to my stomach. "Fuck, I can't even think about that."

Her hand comes to rest on my shoulder. "I know."

"No, you don't. She's not your kid," I say, even though I know that's not fair.

Binx isn't Sprout's parent, but she loves her. She would do anything for her, a fact she proved this past winter when she moved heaven and earth to help us raise the money to pay for Sprout's surgery.

"Sorry," I mutter.

"It's okay," she says, rubbing her palm in slow circles between my shoulder blades. "You're right. I have no idea what it's like to be a parent, but I do know what it's like to be a kid who doesn't fit in. As grown-ups, we know that's not the end of the world, and that misfit kiddos will find their people eventually. But at eight or nine, when everyone else has a bestie, and you're the girl who collects bugs and plays soccer harder than the boys and never knows when to shut her mouth...it can be rough. You start to think there's something wrong with you, that you'll always be the one who doesn't fit in. And I didn't even have the challenges Sprout has right now."

I stretch my neck to one side, fighting to release some of the tension in my jaw.

Binx is right. My daughter was born hearing, but the accident that killed her mother when she was little left her with severe head trauma. She lost her hearing at three, at a pivotal moment, when so much of a kid's skill with language is forming. Then, I wasted so much time grieving that we didn't even get on the list for the children's hospital that specializes in hearing loss surgery until she was five. She had hearing aids, but they didn't do much. She did speak some, but heading into elementary school, she mostly used sign language to communicate.

By the time we realized how much of the surgery *wouldn't* be covered by insurance, she was seven and we were scrambling to raise the money before she lost any more time. She had the procedure last March, recovering seventy percent of her hearing in her left ear and fifty percent in her right. She was finally able to hear music and her grandmother's laugh and, for the first time in years, her own voice.

Seeing as she's one crazy perceptive kid, she immediately realized that it didn't sound "normal," not like the other kids. A period of severe self-consciousness followed. That was only made worse when her best friend, Francesca, moved away, and a few of the meaner kids starting teasing her when she mispronounced words in class.

She's been struggling at school ever since, her grades falling as she becomes more and more withdrawn. She talks nonstop at home, showcasing her crazy vocabulary and sharp mind, but she refuses to participate in class. Even assurances from her speech therapist that she's making amazing progress haven't made a difference. My daughter is determined not to expose her vulnerable underbelly again and regularly asks to be reunited with the sign language interpreter who used to accompany her to her classes.

But the state won't pay for an assistant now that her hearing has been restored. After so much sacrifice and struggle to make it happen, the surgery we'd hoped would make things easier for her, actually seems to have made them harder.

Maybe hard enough that she felt she didn't have much to lose by hitching a ride on a dark rural highway...

I run a hand down my face, fighting a sudden wave of emotion.

"Come here," Binx says, wrapping her arms around me. I stiffen, intending to pull away, but then she curls her fingers around the back of my neck and whispers, "Take the hug, asshole, you need it," and I exhale a rough laugh, my arms wrapping around her curvy little body.

She's one of the most muscular women at our gym, with biceps many a teen boy would envy, but compared to me, she's still a tiny thing. I'm enormous. Always have been. By ten, I was taller than most of my teachers. By twenty, I was the kind of big—six-six and muscled all over —that made people turn to stare when I passed them on the street. Even if I'd wanted to, there was nowhere for someone as big as I am to hide.

So, I learned to put on a brave face, to pretend I didn't mind the stares or whispers that I looked "scary." I faked it until I made it, and the attention no longer bothered me. I know Sprout will eventually learn to do the same—she's a tough kid—but watching her struggle is painful.

Binx is right, I don't want to do anything to add to her pain, no matter how badly she scared me tonight.

"How about this," Binx murmurs, her lips brushing my jawline as she speaks, making me keenly aware of her soft mouth and how much I want to bruise it with mine. "I'll discreetly fetch Sprout from the dance floor and bring her here for a chat. Then you two can decide what happens from there."

"All right," I murmur, my chest aching with longing.

I want to tighten my arms around her, to pull her so close there's not a millimeter between us. I want to run my hands down her back to cup her round ass in my hands and tell her about the many filthy dreams I've had about her. I want to tell her that she's my potty-mouthed angel, my best friend, and that I don't want to imagine my life without her in it.

Which is even more reason to get out of here before I do something stupid with Binx that we can never come back from.

If she shifts forward even half an inch, she's going to feel the erection growing behind the fly of my jeans and know I'm not as immune to the chemistry between us as I've pretended to be for the past two years.

Swallowing hard, I force my hands from around her and step back with a curt nod. "Okay. I'll try to think of a way to get through to her without graphic descriptions of what predators do to little girls."

Binx winces. "Yeah, don't do that. Let her have a few more years of not knowing how awful things are. She's having a hard enough time already." She takes a step backwards, aiming a finger at my chest, "And call your mom while I'm gone. I'm sure Bettie's losing her mind waiting for an update."

I curse, my shoulders tensing again. "Fuck, you're right. I need to tell her to call the cops, too. They were putting out an APB for any sign of Sprout."

Binx nods, her eyes widening. "Yeah, do that. For sure."

She turns, hurrying away while I pull my cell from my back pocket and tap Mom's contact button. She's so relieved that she starts hyperventilating, and I have to talk her into a chair to catch her breath.

By the time I end the call, Binx and Sprout are crossing the grass.

The second I see my daughter's wide, worried eyes, all my angry words are out the window. I crouch down, extending my arms. She runs into them, and I hug her close, so grateful that she's okay.

"I love you," I tell her, still struck by the fact that I don't have to pull back so she can read my lips or watch me sign the words.

She can hear me, even with her face buried in my neck, a fact she proves by squeezing me tighter and whispering, "I'm sorry, Daddy. I know I did a bad thing. I just wanted to go to the party so much."

I stand, lifting her into my arms, letting her feet dangle. "I know, but you can't ever do anything like this again, kid. You could have been hit by a car and killed on the highway or worse." Binx widens her eyes behind Sprout, and I soften my tone as I add, "Hitchhiking is very dangerous. Not all strangers are nice. I don't even hitchhike, and I'm the biggest man I know."

Sprout shoots me a confused look. "I didn't hitch-hike, Daddy."

I frown. "Then how did you get here so fast? There's no way you walked from Grammy's all the way up to the winery before she noticed you were gone."

Her lips quirk up as she snorts. "No, I called a taxi. Mr. Hamish's taxi, the one that comes to the bar when people aren't safe to drive. I called him from Grammy's phone while she was feeding the cats. She always takes her shower after, so I knew she wouldn't be there when he pulled up."

I narrow my eyes on her face. "Clever."

She smiles.

"And bad," I emphasize, wiping the smile away. "But not as bad as hitchhiking."

She nods soberly, making her slightly crooked pigtails bob. She has my wavy brown hair and her mother's green eyes. She also has my height—she's the tallest girl in third grade—but was spared my big, beefy frame. She's a beauty, and is going to be absolutely stunning when she grows up.

I hope I'm always there to protect her from the bad people who are drawn to beautiful girls and women, but if for some reason, I'm not, it's comforting to know she has a good head on her shoulders.

"You realize you scared Grammy to death," I add, making her lips turn down at the edges.

"I know," she says, sounding ashamed. "I was going to leave her a note, but I was afraid she'd come get me before I had time to dance and get cake."

I sigh. "Dancing and cake aren't as important as being

good to the people we love. Scaring Grammy like that wasn't nice. When she called to tell me you were gone, she was crying so hard I could barely understand her at first."

Sprouts eyes widen and begin to shine. "I didn't think she'd be *that* scared. Sometimes I go outside to play without asking."

"Not at nine o'clock at night," I remind her. "And not when you're actually planning to jump into a cab, so she can't find you when she looks outside."

Her bottom lip trembles. "I was pretending I was Cinderella getting in the pumpkin to go the ball. I was just playing. I didn't mean to hurt Grammy's feelings."

"Of course you didn't," Binx says, stepping closer. "And now you'll know never to do anything like this again."

"Is Grammy mad?" Sprout asks, tears slipping from the edges of her eyes.

"No, she was scared. Really scared. Now, she's really glad you're all right." I sigh, adding against my better judgement, "And she wants you to bring her home a piece of wedding cake."

Sprout blinks. "We...we can stay until they cut the cake?"

"We can," I say. "But then we're headed straight home, and you're grounded for a month. No garage sales on Saturday mornings with Grammy or ice cream after school and you'll be doing chores around the new camp to make up for giving me a heart attack."

She nods, a smile curving her lips. "I can do that. I'm a good helper, and I spent all my garage sale money anyway, so I have to save up." She glances at Binx before turning back to me and asking shyly, "Does this mean I can go dance some more, too? Just until it's time for cake? My new friends said they're going to play Come On Eileen soon because they always do that at McGuire parties."

"One of your favorites," I say, though I can't stomach the tune myself. I shake my head and hug her one last time before setting her back on her feet. "Okay. Go, dance. But don't leave the tent," I add. "I want you where I can see you."

"My sister Wendy Ann is in the tent, too," Binx calls after her retreating form. "She's the one with glasses and the boring black dress. Say hi if you see her. She's great and likes math even more than you do."

Sprout spins, flashing us a thumbs-up and a gap-toothed grin. "Roger Dodger."

Then she scampers away, leaving me alone with Binx, her sexy sweater, and sexier bra. And thanks to the adrenaline-fueled evening, my defenses are lower than they've ever been before.

I should head into the tent with Sprout. I should find a place to sit in a corner somewhere and bide my time until the cutting of the cake. Staying here with this woman who smells like wild roses and honeysuckle and looks at me like she wants to have *me* for dessert is a bad idea.

But when Binx asks, "Wanna climb a tree and hide from everyone while we wait?" I say, "Yes," without missing a beat.

Because I'm a feral creature at heart, who never feels more at home than when I'm up a tree, climbing a rock face, or walking through a forest, miles from the nearest human being.

I like being alone. It's why—as soon as my wildlife adventure tour business started making serious bank—I farmed out the task of leading the tours to my employees. I design, organize, and promote the tours, but I let the guides on payroll do the peopling. Once I have the camp running smoothly, I'll do the same there. I'll hire staff to run the wilderness retreat center and only go there myself on weeks when no one has rented it out.

My mother says I have a pathological aversion to humanity, always have, ever since I was a kid. But Binx isn't one of the humans I want to escape from. She's one of the few who make a moment shared with her better than time spent alone. Peace is good, but a connection like this is addictive.

It's like fire, so warm and wonderful that you don't realize the flames have jumped out of the pit and are setting your life ablaze until it's too late.

Fire lingers in my thoughts as I give Binx a boost up to the tree's first large limb, unable to ignore how good it feels to have my hands wrapped around her waist. I'm definitely playing with fire, crawling up into the darkness with this woman, but I can't seem to force myself to turn around.

Sprout came by her wild streak honestly.

And the thought of spending the next half hour alone with Binx is too seductive to resist.

Chapter 3

Wendy Ann McGuire

*A logical woman currently
thinking very illogical thoughts...*

I stand, watching from behind a flower arrangement at the edge of the tent as Binx's crush hoists her into a tree and climbs up after her, my wheels turning.

I'm sure many people would find it strange that a fully grown woman is climbing a tree at a wedding reception, but that's just Binx. She's always danced to the beat of her own drum.

And now she's found a man who hears the same rhythm, a man who clearly adores his daughter and has so much love to give in that big, burly heart of his. A man who also happens to look at my sister like she's the missing variable needed to solve his equation...

"They clearly belong together," I mutter.

"I know, but they don't get it. We have to do something," comes a whisper from my left. I flinch in surprise and spin to see a little girl beside me.

It's Sprout, Seven's daughter. I recognize the description of her dress.

She lifts her hands into the air. "Sorry, didn't mean to scare you. Binx told me to say hi. You're Wendy Ann, right? Her sister?"

"Yes. And you're Sprout."

"Sophia is my real name, but everyone calls me Sprout. You can, too." She flashes a charming, dimpled grin with a hint of mischief around the eyes. "Especially if you want to help with my mission."

I frown. "Your mission..."

She nods. "To get Dad and Binx together. They're already more in love than Flynn Rider and Rapunzel, the best couple there ever was, so it should be easy."

I grunt softly. "Tangled is one of my favorite movies."

Her smile widens. "I knew it."

"Knew what?"

"I knew you were smart. I could tell from your eyes. Smart people have bouncy eyes that never stop moving."

"That could also be a neurological condition."

She arches a brow. "Do you have a neurological condition?" She stumbles a bit on the word "neurological," but she's clearly comfortable with big words, and the slight affectation in her speech is barely noticeable. I remember Binx saying she was having trouble with bullies at school teasing her about the way she talks, but I can't imagine why.

But then again, kids never needed a real reason to bully people when I was in elementary school, either. If they wanted to pick on you, they'd find an excuse, whether it was glasses or reading too much or bringing the same sandwich for lunch every day.

"No," I confess. "I don't."

"I didn't think so," she says. "But you know what you *do* have?"

"What?"

"Time on your hands."

My eyes narrow. "How do you know that? What did Binx say about me?'

"She just said you were smart and liked math, but I could tell you have time on your hands because you're just standing here, spying on other people. Doesn't seem like you have a lot of friends, but that's okay," she says, in a placating tone. "I don't have a lot of friends, either. My best friend moved away, and the rest of the kids at my school are dicks."

My brows shoot up. "Does your dad know you use that word?"

She shrugs. "No. Does Binx know that you spy on her all the time?"

"I don't spy on her all the time, just when she's with a cute boy. I'm a little sister. It's part of the job description," I say, pushing on before she can insult me again. "And what about you? You're spying, too."

An even wider grin bursts across her face. "Exactly! That's why we'll be perfect partners. I've been doing what

I can, but there's only so much a person can do when they can't drive and have to be in boring old school all day."

My lips hook up. As diabolical as this kid is, her grin is contagious. "How old are you?"

"Eight," she says. "But I'm going to be nine in January, and I read at a tenth-grade level. I'm not stupid."

"Clearly," I say. "But neither are they. They'll see a matchmaking scheme coming from a mile away. Especially Binx. And then she'll murder me in my sleep for embarrassing her."

"She won't. She's nice. My dad's nice, too, even though he looks different than other dads."

"He sure does," I mutter, thinking about the way Seven came roaring up the hill on his motorcycle, looking like a bad boy action hero swooping in to save the day.

Speaking of cartoons, his biceps and thighs would give Gaston from Beauty and the Beast a run for his money...

"Ew, gross," Sprout says. "Don't tell me you think my dad's cute, too. The ladies at the playground flirt with him all the time. Keeping them away from him is a full-time job. I barely have any time for the swings." Her nose wrinkles. "And most of them are married, so they should be keeping their giggles and blinky eyes to themselves. Only one of them is a nanny without a husband, but she's even younger than Binx, so I know Dad won't date her."

"Is that the problem?" I ask. "He thinks Binx is too young for him?"

She nods. "Yeah, he's forty-two, which I know is super old, but Binx doesn't care, so why does he?"

"Valid question," I say. "And he doesn't look forty-two. I would have guessed he was in his mid-thirties."

"He takes good care of himself and eats all his vegetables. He also wears sunscreen every day. We put it on together in the bathroom in the mornings, so we don't get skin cancer. He and Grammy and my uncles used to do that when they were kids, too. It's a family tradition."

"It's a good one," I say. "And you seem like a very smart and savvy kid, but—"

"No buts," she cuts in, shaking her head. "Please, you have to help me. I can't ask anyone else, and we have to do something. Fast. Before Dad marries someone he doesn't even love. He has a third date on Friday."

I frown. "So? That doesn't mean he's going to marry someone else."

"He *never* makes it to the third date. I mean *never*, not in my entire life since my mom died. But he and Pammy are going to dinner *and* a movie on Friday. *Pammy*." She makes a gagging face. "That's her name. Do you want me to be cursed with a stepmother named Pammy, Wendy Ann? Is that the kind of awful thing you would put on an innocent kid?"

I cross my arms. "No, of course not, but I honestly don't see what we can do. Your dad has his mind made up, and he seems like a stubborn guy. And I know Binx likes him, but she's a proud person. If she realizes he's getting serious with another woman, that's going to push her away, not make her want to try harder to change his mind."

"But he doesn't love Pammy," Sprout says. "I know he doesn't. He loves Binx, and I do, too. *She* should be part of our family, not some weird stranger with huge boobs and gross yellow Barbie hair."

"Oh wow, Pammy Gore?" I ask as her description brings up a vivid mental picture. "He's dating Pammy Gore?"

"I don't know." She shrugs. "He didn't tell me her last name. I only know what she looks like because she used to come drink at Grammy's bar in the afternoon with her girlfriends. They all wear way too much makeup and laugh like witches, and Pammy's boobs are bigger than my entire head. Each one of them."

I hum. "Yeah, that's Pammy Gore. She went to high school with my older brother, Barrett. She got the implants their senior year. It was a huge scandal."

"It's still a scandal," Sprout mutters. "I'm embarrassed for her."

"You're a funny kid," I say with a huff of laughter.

She scowls. "I know, but I'm not trying to be funny right now. I'm worried. I love Binx so much. Our house feels so cozy and happy when Binx is there. She belongs with us. Even my chickens love her, and Hilda, Henna, and Hermione are very picky. They won't sit and snuggle with anyone except me and Binx." She sighs. "And I know my dad will be so sad later, when Binx marries someone else. He's making a huge mistake, but he won't listen to me about it because I'm just a kid. He told me if I said another word about him dating Binx, he wouldn't invite her over for game night anymore, so I'm completely stuck." She lifts pleading, emerald-green eyes to mine. "If I can't find someone to help me, all of our lives will be ruined."

I shoot her a sympathetic look. "I'm sorry, but—"

"Three lives," she cuts in, her eyes widening. "Maybe four because Pammy will hate being in our family."

"Maybe she won't," I offer, though I still think she's jumping the gun with this Pammy stepmother fear.

"She will," Sprout insists, adding in an ominous tone that's a little disturbing in an eight-year-old, "I plan on being a real pain in the butt to any stepmom who isn't Binx."

I huff again and shake my head. "I see why Binx loves you. You're just like her when she was a kid."

Sprout's face lights up with a joy that makes my heart hurt a little. "Really?"

"Really," I assure her. This kid truly adores my sister, and I know Binx feels the same way. And just from watching Binx and Seven chat beneath the tree for a few minutes, it's clear that they're meant to be. They communicate with the ease of old friends and have the kind of chemistry that gives off sparks in the darkness.

And if age is truly the only barrier...

"So, he has a date Friday night, you said?" I ask, even though I know better.

I can't meddle in Binx's love life. She really *will* kill me. She's a kind, generous big sister who loves me, but she's also independent to a fault. She wants to do everything by herself, with no help from anyone else, especially a bratty little sister who used to steal her clothes and read her text messages while she was sleeping in on Saturday mornings.

"Yes," Sprout says, perking up. "And I know which restaurant and which movie. We can get there first and set booby traps." She chuckles. "Get it? Booby traps? Because Pammy has giant gazoombas?"

I snort. "Yes, I get it. But no, we're not going to booby trap anything. We'll have to set a different kind of trap, one Binx and your dad won't see coming, and that we can deny having any part of if the mission fails."

She nods, her eyes narrowing. "Yeah, that's good. I don't want to get in trouble. I'm already in trouble from tonight." Her brow furrows. "Sometimes I don't think things through as much as I should. It's a problem."

"It's okay," I say gently, falling a little in love with this kid myself. "You're only eight. Your frontal lobe is a long way from being fully developed."

"What's that?" she asks, looking suspicious.

"A part of your brain that deals with executive functions like problem-solving and planning ahead. You'll get better with those things as you get older."

"I'm already smarter than most teenagers," she says. "My cousin Jack does way stupider things than me on a regular basis. He ate laundry detergent one time on a dare and had to go to the hospital. And he never reads anything except captions on the videos on his phone. Grammy says his brain is going to rot straight out his head, and that if she were Uncle Nolan, she would take his phone away until he proved he wasn't an idiot."

"I would, too," I agree. "I wish someone would take my phone away. I hate it, but I can't quit it. I'm too addicted to checking my email."

Sprout nods seriously. "A lot of grown-ups are. That's why my dad is building his retreat center. So people can go there and get away from their phones and stuff. He's going to have a big black box where everyone has to put their phones and computers and they can't get them out again until they leave unless it's an emergency."

"Yeah, Binx mentioned that," I say, my brain cogs catching and spinning in a new direction. "He bought the old Boy Scout camp outside of town, right? The big one?"

"Yeah. It's huge. We have to use a four-wheeler when we're going to the waterfall because it's too far to walk from the cabin."

Cabin...

Hmm....

"I think I have the beginnings of a plan," I say, shushing her when she starts to squeal. "But we have to keep this quiet. The first rule of Parent Trap Club is we don't talk about Parent Trap Club with anyone but each other."

She presses a fist to her mouth, hiding her smile. "Okay, but I'm so excited. I knew you'd help me! I just knew it. We can do this! I know we can!"

"Maybe, with a little luck," I say, my lips curving. "Let's get a piece of cake and discuss things further at one of the tables in the corner, where we won't be overheard."

"Okay, but we'll have to talk fast," she says, following me over to the dessert table, where Tessa and my brother, Wes, are about to cut the first slices of their giant cake. "Dad said we were leaving after cake."

I nod. "Okay. I'll give you my phone number, in case we need to follow up. Do you have a phone?"

She shakes her head. "No, but I can call from the phone at my house or at Grammy's."

"You should use the one at your grammy's. That way your dad won't get suspicious if he looks at his call records and sees a strange number." I pause, reconsidering my words as soon as they're out of my mouth. I turn to her, frowning as I say, "You realize you shouldn't do something like this with any other grown-up ever, right? Not even one you think is nice? I'm a stranger. I could be horrible and awful and dangerous."

She snorts in amusement. "You're not a stranger. You're Binx's sister, and she said you were great and super smart and that I should say hi to you."

"She did?" I ask, touched. I've always thought Binx was great—she's my cool as hell older sister—but I wasn't sure the admiration went both ways.

"She did. And I know not to call weird grown-ups. I'm not stupid."

I twist my lips to one side, still not feeling great about colluding with a child without her parent's knowledge. But considering the nature of our collusion, I can't very well ask Seven for permission to call his kid. "I think we should tell your grammy about our plan," I say, figuring that's a decent compromise. "And if she's on board, then we can move forward."

Sprout groans. "Oh, come on. I'm big enough to call people on my own. And Grammy's going to say no."

"Maybe not. Not if we have a solid plan, and she realizes I'm on board, too. There's strength in numbers."

She grunts. "Maybe. But the plan is going to have to be really good."

"It will be," I assure her with a grin. The more I think about this, the more it seems like it actually might be easy.

I know my sister better than almost anyone, and Sprout and her grandmother know Seven inside and out.

If we can't figure out a way to get these lovebirds out of the tree and on the road to happily ever after, who can?

And what's the worst that can happen?

Binx and Seven don't take the bait and remain "just friends?" That's not so bad. It's just a continuation of the status quo, nothing catastrophic.

Catastrophic...

It's a word that will soon come back to haunt me.

Very, very soon...

Chapter 4

BINX

Monday morning dawns bright and sunny. The sky is blue, the fall leaves in my backyard are vibrant and glorious, and I have my kitchen cleaned and oatmeal muffins in the oven by nine a.m.

Still, I can't shake the feeling that something's wrong.

That I'm forgetting something or overlooking something or...*something*.

"It's because I'm not getting ready for work," I tell Mr. Prickles, my pet thimble cactus.

I love furry pets, but my family has enough crazy animals, and I'm the designated pet sitter for all of them. I wasn't sure I could find a pet that would be okay with occasionally sharing our space with a skunk, a horny squirrel, and a growing flock of turkeys.

Besides, Mr. Prickles is adorable.

And he's a great listener, a fact he proves by continuing to hang on my every word as I explain, "For years and years, I would have been dressed in scratchy business

43

clothes and out the door by now. I just need to learn to relax and enjoy my new schedule."

Lydia, my tattoo mentor and new boss, closes her shop on Sundays, Mondays and Tuesdays, which means I now have a three-day weekend every weekend. I'll also have either Friday night or Saturday night off. That's part of the reason Lydia wanted to take on a partner, so she could go see her husband's band play more often.

I'll have so much more free time than I did before with only a slight decrease in pay, and that should turn around once I build a reputation and start booking regular clients who want larger pieces. I started tattooing actual people instead of melons and oranges about six months ago, but I'm still at the stage of my career where I mostly handle walk-ins and people wanting smaller stuff.

But I have a consult for a giant back piece for my friend, Pierce, from the gym next week. If he decides to go for it, that'll be a bump in income for at least the next few months. With tattoos of that size, you can't complete everything in one visit. You have to give the skin time to heal in between. Even the sleeve on my arm, which is much smaller than Pierce's back, took three, five-hour sittings to get everything just right.

But it was so worth it. I love my tattoo, with the flowers swirling around my bicep and the skull tucked beneath pink-and-yellow peony petals.

My mother, however, hates the skull with the same fervor with which she loves Jane Fonda. She hates tattoos in general, but the skull really took it over the edge for her. Even when I explained that it was a memento mori— a reminder of death fine art painters have been incorporating into their work for centuries—she insisted I should have it removed.

She said it was "tacky and masculine and morbid."

But I think being reminded of death every time I glance down at my arm is a good thing. It reminds me not to waste a minute of the precious life I've been given.

Which reminds me...

Grabbing my phone, I collect Mr. Prickle's from his position on the shelf above the sink and head outside to soak up some autumn sun while weighing my options.

"On the one hand, it's a big expense," I say, setting Mr. Prickles in the center of my outdoor table before curling into a cushioned chair and drawing my thick robe tighter around me. It's barely fifty degrees, but I know winter will be here before I know it, and coffee on the back porch will be a thing of the past until spring. "But on the other hand, it's thirty percent off."

I turn my cell, showing him the email that popped into my inbox last night. It's from a company offering rock-climbing tours that I started following a few years ago, mostly to support Wendy Ann's friend, Lilac, who started the venture right after college. Part of what I love most about rock climbing is the chance to be alone with my thoughts or in the company of one or two good climbing friends. The thought of joining a ten-to-twelve-person tour, with no idea who I'm going to be stuck in close quarters with for three days isn't a selling point for me.

But I've been dying to check out the Golden Spire bluffs down south, and they're on private land. The area is only accessible through a tour or by making reservations over a year in advance.

"Thirty percent off, and I could mark the bluffs off my list without having to plan ahead," I tell Mr. Prickles. "You know I hate planning ahead."

Mr. Prickles chuckles a little at that.

What can I say? He knows me.

But Wendy Ann knows me even better and Lilac, the owner of Rock Out Climbs, is one of her best friends. If anyone can get the "behind the scenes" scoop for me, it will be my little sis.

I punch Wendy Ann's contact on my phone and put my cell to my ear, not surprised when she answers after the first ring. "Good morning, sunshine," I say in response to her cranky-sounding hello. "How's Monday treating you so far?"

"Mom woke me up at four-thirty doing aerobics over my head," she says. "And I haven't heard back about any of the applications I put in last week."

"It's still early. Just relax and do something to keep your mind off the waiting. Like, say... Oh, I don't know, maybe a favor for your favorite sister."

She harrumphs. "You're not my favorite anymore."

"What? Why?"

"You didn't come over for dinner last night," she whines, though I told her that I've been skipping Sunday dinners. It's just easier not to fight with Mom if I'm not around her all that much. "I was alone with Mom and Dad and all our happily married siblings. It was awful. I felt like a third wheel times ten."

"We only have six married siblings. Plus Mom and

Pops, that's seven. Seven happy couples, mwuah-ha-ha," I say, doing my best Count impression from Sesame Street.

"Well, it felt like ten, and half of them were cranky and hungover from the wedding reception and the other half were giving the first half shit for being hungover. And then Christian cheated at Monopoly and Mel pounced on him like a spider monkey and Freya the ferret tried to bite his balls because she thought he was a threat. Then Keanu Reeves got into the garbage again while we were all distracted."

"That dog and garbage," I mutter. "He has a problem."

"He does," she agrees. "He ate something that made his butt smell terrible and got one of the foil wrappers from our baked potatoes stuck on his head. Barrett and I had to chase him around the pasture for almost an hour to get it off. It was exhausting." She sighs. "I didn't get to sleep until almost eleven for the second night in a row."

I hum sympathetically. "Poor thing. Being expected to stay up past ten o'clock at the doddering old age of twenty-three? That's awful."

"It *is* awful," she says, but there's laughter in her voice as she adds, "I have to get out of this house and away from Mom's crack-of-dawn exercise fetish before I become even more lame than I am already. I'm going to see if I can find a sublet or something short term to rent until I find out where I'm going to be working. Then I'll worry about explaining my move to Mom and Dad if I find something."

"Sounds smart," I say. "I'll keep my ear to the ground

47

and let you know if I hear of anyone who's looking for a roommate."

"Thank you," she says.

"You're welcome, and you can repay me by calling your friend Lilac and asking who's going on her Golden Spire climbing tour this week, the one that's thirty percent off. I don't start at the tattoo studio until next Wednesday and the good weather is supposed to hold for a while. I'd be interested in joining the fun as long as there aren't any Craigs or Petes on her list."

Wendy Ann laughs. "Craigs or Petes? Why Craigs or Petes? There are way worse names. Chad, for example. Brad and Thad are also bad."

"Agreed, but it's not about the name in general. It's about a particular Craig and Pete who run in the rock-climbing circles around here. They never shut up. It's just a constant, stream-of-consciousness chat fest. And when they're not talking, they're blasting 90's bro rock on their portable speaker. The one and only time I did a climb with them, I wanted to stab my ears out."

"Ah, gotcha," Wendy Ann says. "I'll shoot her a text and ask. Do you want me to have her save you a spot if Craig and Pete *aren't* on the list?"

"Yes, please, that would be great," I say. "Would you want to come, too? I know you don't have a lot of experience with climbing, but I could help you. This climb isn't supposed to be that hard. It's famous for the views and the hot springs along the way, not the difficulty."

"Thanks, but no," she says. "I'm still sore from carrying flowers up to the tent on Saturday."

"You only carried four arrangements. And they were the small ones."

"Exactly. Grad school wasn't great for my physical fitness. The brain is strong, but the muscles are weak." Her voice brightens as she adds, "But I think you'll have a great time. Let me touch base with Lilac and get back to you."

"Okay, thanks," I say, smiling at Mr. Prickles, who seems pleased by this development as well.

Or maybe he's just enjoying the sunshine.

"You're welcome and...Binx?"

"Yeah?" I ask, my ears perking up at her tone. "Everything okay?"

"Yeah, yeah, everything's good. I mean, mostly good. I just...I love you. You know that, right? And that I'm always on your side no matter what?"

Touched, I say, "Yes, weirdo. And same. Oh! If I land a spot on the trip, why don't you come stay at my place while I'm gone? You can get some time away from Mom and Dad, and I know Mr. Prickles would appreciate the company."

She laughs. "Your pet cactus? Is he still alive?"

"Alive and kickin.' Or pricklin', as he likes to say, and he really does enjoy company around the house, so you'd be most welcome."

She snorts. "And you call *me* a weirdo. Have a good day. I'll get back to you as soon as I hear from Lilac. Oh, and don't be late to the shower. They only rented out the bar for two hours, so they want everyone there on time tonight."

I blink faster, sputtering as I hurry to catch her before

she hangs up, "Wait, what? What shower? Tatum isn't due for months. And we already had a shower for Phoebe. Do we have to do one for every baby? Because I think that's going to get excessive. Drew and Tatum like raw dogging way too much."

"Ew. Why do you always find the grossest way to talk about sex?"

I grin. "I do not. I could have said something way grosser. You want to hear?"

"No," she says quickly. "And it's not a baby shower. It's for Starling and Christian." She pauses, adding when I respond with confused silence. "Their combo wedding shower and bachelor/bachelorette party? The one they've been planning for months?"

I frown harder. "What? This is the first I'm hearing about any of this."

"No, it isn't. You said you would bring Jello shots."

I sit up straighter, my stomach sinking as this begins to sound familiar. "Oh no. Was this discussed on poker night back in July?"

"Yes, the one where you took Christian for two hundred bucks and Starling had a fit because the deposit for the bar was due the next day, and they'd just dropped a bunch of money on the wedding venue, too."

I curse.

"I can't believe you forgot," Wendy Ann says.

"Of course I forgot. I was focused on poker. Besides, they should have sent out an event reminder or something."

"They did. Twice. It's in the family group text."

"I left the family group text," I say, standing to pace around the deck. "You know I hate group projects."

"A family text isn't a group project, but I hear you. The notifications are a lot. But you didn't have to leave. You can just mute the conversation and check in on it once every few days or so. That way you stay connected without being bombarded. So, what are you going to do about the Jello shots? Even if you make them right now, they won't be firm by five o'clock, will they?"

"No, they will," I say, dragging a hand down my face as I realize my lazy morning just took a turn for the hectic. "I won't be able to do the layered ones with different colors, but I can get basic shots done. I just have to run to the store for supplies and get my ass in gear. Talk later, okay? At the party, I guess? And will you text me the exact time and address?"

"Will do," Wendy Ann says. "And I'll drop those old bell-bottoms you wore for spirit week in high school in your mailbox on my way to babysit Sara Beth and Phoebe."

My forehead snatches back into a frown. "What? Why?"

"It's a costume party, of course. I mean, it's Christian and Starling, what else would it be? It's a summer of love, hippy theme, and they wanted everyone to prepare a 1970's soft rock classic for karaoke."

I groan. "I mean, I'm all for goofy fun, but 1970's soft rock? What is that even?"

"I don't know. I'm going to google it while I'm watching the girls for Tatum. She's taking a final for her early childhood education class. I should probably head out now, actually. She was hoping to leave early so she would have time to study without Phoebe latched onto her boob. She's struggling with the whole weaning thing, I guess."

"Okay, okay, head out and I'll see you later," I say. "And thanks for dropping those bell-bottoms off. I definitely don't have time for costume hunting at this point."

We say goodbye, and I launch into motion, toting Mr. Prickles back inside before throwing on sweats and a hoodie and jogging out to my truck. I hit the grocery store first, grabbing a few different kinds of Jello and face paint from the Halloween aisle, so I can draw a peace sign on my cheek later and call myself "ready to hippie."

Then, I cruise over to the "bad" side of town—though Bad Dog really doesn't have many rough areas inside the city limits—to the only liquor store open before ten a.m. I'm grabbing lemon vodka and dark rum when I hear a familiar voice from the next aisle over.

"Stop it," the woman coos with a soft trill of laughter. "It's not a big deal, darlin'. I don't mind at all. You know I work just a few doors down from the liquor store. I'll bring the vodka and other stuff over this afternoon around four, when I'm done with my last client. Tell your mama not to worry."

I duck down, discreetly peeking through the space between the shelves, to see massive breasts straining the front of a bright pink sweater, and wrinkle my nose.

Yep, it's Pammy, all right.

Pammy, who worked as a touring stripper for ten years before returning home to open a hair and tanning salon.

Pammy, who looks like she escaped from a 1980s rock video, complete with the orange tan and frosted blue eye shadow.

Pammy, who is as hyperfeminine as I am "just one of the guys" and who was spotted at Bubba Jump's with Seven a few weeks back. Maybe it was a date, maybe it wasn't, but my friend, Zan, told me Pammy was using Seven's body like a stripper pole, and that there was zero room for the Holy Spirit between her boobs and his face.

Now she's cooing to someone on the phone about dropping off vodka for his "mama" this afternoon...

I only know one person who would need the extra-large bottles she's shifting into her cart—Bettie. Which means she was talking to Seven, and she just called him "darlin'."

Fighting a wave of physical sickness, I stand up, pressing a fist to my mouth.

No. No, no, no! This can't be happening. Seven can't be falling for Pammy. I mean, Pammy is okay, I guess, but she's not right for him. Not even close. She spends way too much time on primping and makeup and hair, and there's no way she could rock climb or lift weights with nails that long. Working on fixing up motorcycles is out, too. She wouldn't want to get her soft little hands dirty.

Maybe that's what he likes about her, that she's not a dude with boobs.

"I am not a dude with boobs," I mutter beneath my breath, torn between slinking away and staying to eaves-drop. A part of me is dying for further clues as to what exactly is happening between Seven and Pammy, but the other part doesn't want to know.

What if he tells her he loves her?

What if she says it back?

How will I ever be okay again? And how could Seven even *think* about developing feelings for someone else when we spent twenty minutes in a tree together Saturday night sharing our favorite tree house memories from when we were kids? After he laughed at my story and ruffled my hair, and then the hair ruffle turned into his face moving closer to mine and another almost-kiss that left me breathless?

He loves *me*, not Pammy. I know that the way I know that lemon vodka elevates a yellow Jello shot and that rum is the only choice for the cherry ones.

"Aw, you're so welcome, sweetheart. Yeah, you too," Pammy says. "See you soon."

Sweetheart...

It's not the "L" word, but it's way too close for comfort.

I have to do something. I have to take action now, before it's too late.

After checking out, I hurry to my truck with my supplies, a plan serving itself up on a silver platter as a text from Wendy Ann pops through on my dashboard. The digital voice reads her message, assuring me that there will be no losers on the tour and that my space is reserved.

When the A.I. asks if I want to respond, I say yes, and ask—"Is there room for one more? I might see if Seven wants to go."

Wendy Ann doesn't respond right away, but I assume that's because she's following up with Lilac, or wrangling children, and put it out of my mind. It isn't until I show up at the shower dressed in skintight orange and brown bell-bottoms that smell of moth balls to see Seven behind the bar with Bettie mixing drinks, that I remember my plan.

I wonder why he didn't mention that he was bartending at my brother's shower, but there's no time to get to the bottom of that mystery right now. I head off to find my sister, wanting to know if there's room on the tour before I mention it to Seven—preferably in front of Bettie, who I know will offer to babysit. She's always telling him that he works too hard and needs to make time to play while he's still young enough to do the grueling physical things he enjoys.

I don't think Seven is running out of time for that anytime soon—he's in incredible shape, proven by the number of women ogling him as they flip through the karaoke app looking for songs—but I'm not above using Seven's mom fears to my advantage.

And I'm not above packing my skimpiest bikini for the hot springs while Seven and I are off on that climbing trip.

Or maybe I'll forget my bikini altogether and go with some lacy lingerie...

If I'm going to make one last play for Seven before he's snatched up in the gravitational pull of Pammy's giant boobs, I intend to make it a serious one.

Chapter 5

SEVEN

I know the second she steps into the bar.

Before I turn to look.

Before she's said a word or slipped into my peripheral vision.

I don't know how I know—her perfume isn't strong enough to carry the distance between us—but I just *know*. Where Binx McGuire is concerned, I have a sixth sense, and even though she doesn't come over to say hello, I never lose track of where she is.

First, she drops a tray of Jello shots with Starling and her friends, who welcome the delivery with a cheer and a chorus of giggles. Then, she stops to speak to Wendy Ann, who's hiding out by the snack table. Wendy Ann glances my way for a moment, but averts her gaze a second later, and when they're done speaking, Binx doesn't head my way. She pulls her phone from her small purse, texts something in response to whatever message she received, and starts for the back door.

She doesn't so much as glance my direction before

stepping into the beer garden that's always a big draw in the summer.

But it's closed now, and Chip, the bar manager, made us promise not to let anyone take drinks outside. He's already put away the plasticware for the season and doesn't want to deal with broken glass on the cobbled paving stones.

Binx didn't have a glass, but when she doesn't come back inside for several moments, I start to wonder what she's up to.

Then I start to worry...

Because that's what I do when it comes to Binx, even though she's one of the strongest, most capable people I know.

It's another sign that I *shouldn't* cancel my date with Pammy for this weekend, even if I'm pretty sure there's no long-term potential there. But Pammy's a nice person, easygoing and fun, and she seems cool with taking things slow. Besides, the more I invest in other relationships, the less I'll find myself turning to Binx.

I've let things with us get too close, too intense...

I almost kissed her again at the wedding, and I've been having dreams about stripping that see-through sweater off her with my teeth ever since.

I shouldn't go check on her. She's fine. She's a big girl and the beer garden is fenced in. Literally nothing could have happened to her back there. I'm being overprotective.

I make another Bette Davis, Mom's signature drink, and grit my teeth through the first karaoke performance, a John Denver number, crooned by Binx's father, that reminds me way too much of Binx. It's Annie's Song, a ballad for Denver's wife that talks about the way she "fills up his senses, like a night in the forest." It's so close to what Binx does to me—especially when we're on a climb or taking our mountain bikes out on the trails—that it hurts a little.

It also makes me scan the room again for Binx, but there's no sign of her. She must still be outside...but why?

I know she isn't a huge fan of karaoke, but she loves her brother and according to the monitor, Christian is due onstage in a couple more songs.

"I'm going to run to the men's room, Mom," I murmur after she's pushed two Marilyn Monroes across the bar. "Can you swing it alone for a few minutes?"

"Of course, I can," she says, with a huff. "I'm a professional, baby. Take your time and mingle a little bit after. I've got this, and you've been working way too hard."

I give a non-committal grunt and duck under the bar at the far end. Nodding hello to Tessa, the one who called this morning, begging Mom to fill in for the bartender who bailed on the event last minute, I bypass the restrooms and head straight outside.

Moving past the whiskey barrel planters, where a few withering mums fight for survival amongst a knot of weeds, I step onto the large open patio, expecting to find Binx talking on her phone or something. But she's nowhere to be seen. I frown and spin in a slower circle, searching the trees by the fence for signs of a feminine leg dangling from the branches, but she isn't up a tree, either.

She's also not behind the wood panel concealing the

dumpsters or in the smoking area. The last part, I'm glad about—I've been giving her shit for smoking clove cigarettes for months, even though she only has one or two a week—but still...

Where the hell is she?

I'm about to jump the fence to check the other side, when I hear a low chuckle and a man's voice murmuring, "Fuck, woman, that tickles. Your fingers are freezing." It sounds like the guy's around the corner, so I move in that direction, spotting the back entrance to the kitchen just as a woman's voice says, "Yeah, well, it's October, dude. Get used to it. Only going to get colder from here on out. Now hold still."

My ears perk up and a scowl claws into my forehead.

That was Binx. I would know her voice anywhere.

But what the hell is she doing hanging out in the kitchen with some dude in the middle of her brother's wedding shower? And why is she touching him with her "freezing fingers?"

"I'm serious," she adds with a husky chuckle, "the more you wiggle, the longer this is going to take, and we don't have much time."

The more he wiggles?

What the actual fuck?

Is the seeing someone? Or just...fucking around? Fucking around with someone she likes enough to give him a hand job while her entire family is in the next room?

"I'm not wiggling, I'm just ticklish," comes the male voice, bringing a full-fledged snarl to my lips. "You know that. Even when you were sticking it in me for the little one, I couldn't stop laughing."

Sticking it in him? Sticking *what* in him?

And what the hell is Binx doing with some thin-skinned, ticklish motherfucker who wants her to stick things in him? That's not what Binx wants in a lover. I would bet every acre of my hard-won land on that.

We've obviously never slept together, but her eyes tell me she wants to be pushed up against a wall and taken by a man who's not afraid to show her what she does to him. She wants to be held down hard while she gives as good as she gets. She wants passion and intensity from an equal, not some wimp who can't make it through a hand job without getting a case of the giggles.

"Oh baby, yeah," he says, giggling like a psychopath. "Scribble on that back fat."

The words don't make sense, but it doesn't matter. They still make me see red—vibrant, crazy-making red. The next thing I know, I'm charging through the door into the back of the kitchen, expecting to encounter Binx getting it on with some employee of the bar.

What would I have done if my expectations had been met?

I have no idea.

Getting jealous and possessive with a woman I've pushed away with both hands wouldn't have been cool. It would have been a dick move, and I do my best not to be a dick, especially to the women in my life. Women put up with enough shit from the male population, and I have a daughter. I'm very invested in being a good example to other men as to how the feminine half of the species should be treated—namely, with respect.

And it isn't respectful to interfere with a friend's sexual choices, even if they are making those choices mere feet from a family function, where their father was recently singing 70's soft rock.

But Binx isn't giving a chef a hand job or feeling up a dishwasher. No, she's...drawing. Drawing on Pierce Livermore, the owner of The Whiskey Bar and Grill, a regular at our gym, and the guy I call Liver*wurst* behind his back because he's the worst.

He's the kind of guy who spends half his workout taking selfies in the mirror, never cleans the equipment after he's sweated all over it, and—worst of all—stands around naked after his shower, making small talk about the latest NHL game with his saggy balls dangling down to mid-thigh. He also talks shit about women, usually about the college girls who come to lift while they're on break, but he's made repulsive comments about Binx before, too.

Of course, that was before I glared him down at the sinks and told him to keep her name out of his mouth.

Since then, he's been well-behaved when it comes to my best friend.

Or so I thought...

Right now, he isn't behaving himself. When I burst through the door, he's craning his neck to stare at Binx's ass in her skintight bell-bottoms, while she doodles on him with a Sharpie, too engrossed in her work to realize he's being a pervert.

Then, she's too shocked by me bursting through the door.

"Oh my God, what the fuck?" she says, surging to her feet so fast that she hits Pierce's chin with the top of her head and they both curse in pain.

"I heard you talking and thought you were in trouble," I blurt out, catching a glimpse of what looks like a pirate ship on Pierce's back before he tugs his shirt down.

"No, I'm fine. Jesus. Sorry about smashing your face," she says to Liverwurst, touching a hand to his chest.

I instantly want to snatch her hand away and spray it down with hand sanitizer, and that's before Pierce flexes, making his pecs jump beneath his long-sleeved t-shirt.

"It's okay," he says, rubbing his chin with one hand as he touches the side of her waist with the other.

"No, it's not. Hands off," I snap, the words out of my mouth before I can think better of them.

Instantly, I know I've fucked up, but even *I'm* not prepared for the suddenness of the storm that sweeps into Binx's eyes.

"What?" she demands, in a tone that makes it clear, the word isn't a question. It's a statement on my epic tomfoolery.

I lift my hands in surrender and take a breath. "I just meant..." I trail off, my thoughts spinning, sending up sprays of thought gravel.

What did I mean? *What?* My improvisational skills aren't great at the best of times, and these are not the best of times. Not with Pierce standing there looking all smug and expectant, like a kid about to watch his bully get pummeled under the bleachers.

But I'm not the bully here—he is. He's the one who talked about Binx's "rack" and how he wouldn't mind "tapping that ass" even though, at the time, she didn't have any hair to grab, while he was "giving it to her" from behind. But I can't very well call him out on that to his face, not in front of Binx. We all go to the same gym and run in the same social circles and Bad Dog is a small town. Spilling the dirt like this would make things uncomfortable for all of us.

I have to think of something else to say.

Some reasonable excuse.

Think, asshole, think! For fuck's sake.

But I've got nothing.

Nothing but one ridiculous idea, it looks like I'm going to have to run with...

Chapter 6

SEVEN

"Contamination," I finally blurt out, wincing a little.

It's lame, so fucking lame, but I've already started down this path, and there's no turning back now.

"I was worried about...food contamination," I continue, feeling my cheeks heat as I continue to pull nonsense out of my ass. "If Pierce is prepping food, he shouldn't get his um..." I pull in a breath, wishing I could turn back time and think of something, *anything* less stupid to say. "Shouldn't get his hands dirty," I finish in a softer voice as Binx looks at me like I've grown a second head that speaks exclusively in pig Latin.

"There's a sink right there, dude." Pierce nods to the wall behind Binx as he studies me with an expression that's both amused and pitying. "And I'm done with the prep anyway. I just have to pull the wieners off the grill."

"Right, I... Well, that's good," I say, wishing I had an excuse to punch him.

I *really* want to punch him.

So much.

The urge only gets worse when Binx pats his chest with an easy affection and says, "You should do that, Pierce. I'm sure the savages will be hungry for more than chips soon. But take a look at the area I roughed-in when you get the chance. See if that's big enough. We can always go bigger if you want, but I think this size will give it a nice feeling of movement without showing above your collar when you put on a dress shirt and pretend to be a corporate douchebag."

"Aw, thanks," Pierce says, shooting a smirk my way. "But it's not pretend. I *am* a corporate douchebag. I've already sold three franchises for Chickie Fingers, one of them in Iowa. Pretty soon, I'll be nationwide."

"That's awesome, douchebag, congrats," she says, summoning a snort of laughter from Pierce as she moves toward me.

"You're a character, McGuire," he says to her back.

Or to her ass, rather. As soon as she turned away, he was right back to ogling her like a piece of meat. There's a way to appreciate a woman's body without looking like a cartoon wolf drooling over a turkey leg, but Pierce hasn't mastered the craft. Not even close.

But before I can say something I shouldn't—again— Binx grabs a fistful of my sweatshirt and mutters, "Come with me. I need to talk to you about something."

"Yeah, me, too," I say, glaring at Pierce's smug ass face one last time before following her outside.

I warn him with my eyeballs that this isn't over, and

that I'm not going to let him sneak into Binx's affections through the tattoo studio's back door.

He glares back, his eyeballs telling me that he isn't going through the back door, he's going through the front, and there's nothing I can do about it. Then he makes a gross joke about enjoying "back door action" that makes me want to punch him again.

And yes, I'm aware that eyeballs don't actually talk, and I'm imagining all of this, but it feels real.

As real as the heat in Binx's tone as she drags me into the shade by the fence and hisses, "What was that about, Seven?" I pull in a breath, but she cuts me off before I can speak. "If you say anything about contamination, I swear, I'm going to lose it."

I exhale, knowing better than to try to come up with a lie.

I don't lie to Binx. At least, I try not to. I withhold sometimes, I evade, but I don't lie.

"I'm sorry," I say instead, keeping my voice low. "But I know Pierce. He's an asshole with zero respect for women."

Her scowl doesn't waiver. "Yeah, I know."

My brows lift. "You know? And you're still interested?"

"No, I'm not interested." She rolls her eyes with a huff. "He's a client, Seven. A client who wants a very large, very pricey tattoo that will keep me in work for months."

I grunt. "And keep you in close quarters with a man who's said raunchy, demeaning shit about you behind your back."

"So?" She folds her arms over her chest. "It wouldn't be the first time, and I'm sure it won't be the last. At least this way I'll be getting paid while he stares at my boobs."

I prop my hands on my hips, shaking my head. "You don't understand. Pierce isn't just your average creep. He's fucking gross. After you shaved your head, he kept talking about how he wouldn't have anything to hold onto while he...you know."

She sighs, still looking spectacularly unimpressed. "While he what? Gave it to me good?"

I shrug uncomfortably. "In a grosser turn of phrase, but yeah. And he said it in the middle of the locker room at the gym, surrounded by people he knows are your friends. He has zero respect for you."

"I don't care if he respects me," she says. "I'm never going to date him. I'm just going to tattoo his skin with permanent ink so he'll bear the giant mark of the woman who refused to fuck him for the rest of his life." Her eyes glitter and her lips hook up on one side. "So, who gets the last laugh, Seven? You tell me."

My shoulders slump. I know when I've been defeated, but that doesn't mean I have to like it. "I'm still going to be worried."

"I'll be fine. I can handle Pierce."

"But what if you can't?" I press. "You're tough but he's got half a foot and at least seventy pounds on you."

"I can take him."

"No, you can't," I insist. "He's almost as big as I am, and I could pick you up and throw you across the room with one hand."

She rolls her eyes and mutters something I can't make out beneath her breath.

"What was that?" I ask.

"Nothing," she says. "I should go. I've already missed too much of the karaoke. Someone's going to get offended if I don't go join in the 'fun.' See you inside."

"Tell me what you said. Please," I say, curling my fingers around her elbow when she tries to leave.

Instantly, electricity shivers up my arm. My stomach tightens, warmth floods through my core, and all I want to do is pull her closer. I want to tuck her under my chin, wrap my arms tight around her, and growl at anyone who dares to get close to what's mine.

But she's not mine, and she never will be.

I have to let her go. I have to leave her alone so she can find someone capable of giving her the love, support, and protection I can't. But not Pierce. I can't leave her alone with him, not even as a client.

I'm about to volunteer to be her bodyguard during her appointments with the jerk, when Binx bursts out, "I said, 'but you wouldn't.' You wouldn't pick me up with one hand because you don't ever put your hands on me. Even at the wedding, as soon as you gave me a boost into the tree, you couldn't let go fast enough. I almost fell because I didn't have a good grip on the branch yet."

I shake my head. "I'm sorry, I—"

"I don't want you to be sorry, I want you to tell me why you really said what you said back there." She steps closer, until her sweet, sexy smell fills my head. "Why did you tell Pierce to get his hands off me? Why were you glaring at him like you wanted to smash his face in with a rusty tire iron?"

I swallow and curl my hands into fists.

I won't touch her.

I can't.

Even if I could, this isn't the time and certainly not the place. Her entire family is inside, not to mention my mother. If we were going to give dating a try, it would have to be something we kept quiet. I wouldn't want my mother or Sprout to get excited about something that might not work, and it's obvious her parents think I'm trash. Getting involved with an ex-con, no matter how long ago I served my time, would only make her relationship with them more strained.

I don't want that for her.

Especially not for something that wouldn't last.

But it would last. That's the problem. She doesn't mind that you're intense as fuck and color outside the lines. You're perfect for each other. At least for now. You'd draw her in, tie her down, and use her up. By the time she realizes she threw her youth away on an old man, it'll be too late. You'll be a grandpa and she'll be stuck trying to find another partner in middle age, a thing you know sucks all the fucking ass.

Or you'll be dead, and she'll be alone.

The men in my family don't live long, healthy lives. The ones who don't self-destruct get taken out by heart disease or lung cancer or some weird twist of fate.

I'll be lucky if I get another twenty years.

In twenty years, Binx will be forty-six, around the same age I am now, and I sure as hell can't imagine myself with a sixty-year-old woman. Hell, my mother's only sixty-eight. But under all the blue dye, her hair is nearly white, and she can't get up off the floor after playing games with Sprout without holding onto the couch.

The aging process between twenty-six and forty-six might not be that big of a deal, but a lot more degeneration happens between forty-six and sixty-six.

I can already feel myself starting to slow down. I can't work a twelve-hour day without a good night's sleep anymore, and I get injured so much more easily than I did as a younger man. I haven't had something major go wrong, but I deal with enough weird, new aches and pains to be irritated with my body on a regular basis. It's only gotten worse since I hit my late thirties. It's enough to make me pretty sure that fifty-two is going to feel a hell of a lot different—and more physically unpleasant—than forty-two.

That's my future. I have maybe ten more good years left, and Binx deserves so much more.

And...so do I. I've worked too damned hard to turn my life around to fuck it up now. I don't want to spend my golden years plagued by guilt or feeling like a selfish bastard or a burden.

My only choice is to walk away and do whatever it takes to get this woman out of my head, even if it means taking Pammy up on her offer to stay at her mother's timeshare in Cancun this December. We haven't done anything more than kiss goodnight at this point, but maybe it's time we should.

Maybe if I start touching someone else, then *not* touching Binx will get easier.

But when she reaches out, grabbing a fistful of my sweatshirt in her hand once again, I don't pull away. I hold my ground as she steps closer, and even the feel of her knuckles against my skin through the cotton is enough to make me hard. "Come on," she murmurs, tilting her chin back to hold my gaze. "Tell me. You have your faults, but I've never known you to be a coward."

"I'm going inside," I tell her, but my hand is already curling around her hip.

"Then go," she says, gripping my shirt with her other hand now, too, holding on tight. I bend closer, until our lips are only inches apart, and I'm practically crawling out of my skin with the need to kiss her.

I want to lift her into my arms, pin her against the fence, and show her exactly why I told Pierce to get his hands off her. It's because I want *my* hands all over her, memorizing every inch of her skin, giving her pleasure, making her scream my name, showing her that she's all I think about these days when I'm alone in bed and reach down the front of my boxer briefs.

I'm about to do it—to let this genie out of the bottle and ruin both of our lives—when a strident voice calls across the patio, "Binx, what are you doing?"

We startle apart, Binx releasing my shirt with a spasm of her hands as we both turn to face the petite woman standing just outside the back door. She has salt-and-pepper brown hair and eyes the same brilliant blue as Binx's.

Fuck, it's her mother. We've never been introduced, but I've seen her around town with her kids and grandkids. She's usually smiling and saying hello to everyone, playing her role as "pillar of the community" to the hilt.

But she's not smiling now. She's looking at Binx like she's a naughty child and I'm a pile of dog shit she's been playing in while the grown-ups were distracted.

"Nothing," Binx says with a rush of breath. She flaps a hand toward the kitchen door. "I was just talking to Pierce about his tattoo while he finished up the barbeque, and then Seven said he might...want something."

Her mother scowls. "Want something?"

"Yeah, a tattoo. A, um, a flower or a bee or something. What was it you said you wanted? I'm sorry, I've been running around like a crazy person all day making Jello shots." She glances up at me with a "thinking face" that looks nothing like her real thinking face.

She's a terrible actor, and her mother isn't buying any of this, but I nod anyway and say, "A bee, yeah. Maybe with blackberries around it. I thought we could weave it into my sleeve on my left arm."

Binx hums a little too loudly. "Oh yeah, that's right. Sure, we can totally do that. Just come by the shop next Wednesday night. That's when I have apprentice hours."

Apprentice hours...

So, she still hasn't told her mother about changing jobs. And tattooing for a living is a lot less scandalous than dating an older man who spent eighteen months in prison for driving a getaway car, who also has a kid.

"Cool," I say, with a stiff nod. "I'll do that."

Her mother lets out a long-suffering breath. "Well, anyway, your song is up next. We've been looking for you everywhere. I know you aren't a big fan of singing in public, but it means a lot to your brother."

"I know, Mom, I'll be right in, I promise," Binx says, but her mother doesn't budge. She just stands there, glaring at her daughter with increasing disappointment until Binx shoots me an apologetic glance and whispers, "Call me later, we're not done with this discussion," before hurrying across the patio.

But I'm not going to call her later.

I am, in fact, going to ignore her texts for the next five hours before blocking her number.

Then I'm going to call Rob and ask him to cover for me at work while I take my mother up on her offer to watch Sprout while I go on a last-minute, rock-climbing trip for a few days. When she first suggested the trip this morning, I shut her down without hesitation, citing all the shit I have to do to get the cabin renovations finished before winter sets in.

But now...

Now, I need to get the fuck out of town and away from Binx. I need to clear my head, refocus my thoughts, and firm up my resolve. And if I can't do those things, I need to work up the guts to make a clean break. Better to lose a friend than to betray her. I'd rather cut off my own hand than hurt Binx.

I'd do anything for her, in fact, except the one thing she wants.

It's star-crossed as fuck. Even a guy who slept through the ninth-grade unit on Romeo and Juliet can see that.

But I don't see much else. I remain blinded by my own forbidden crush until I'm stranded in the wilderness Tuesday morning with no cell phone, no car, and a creeping suspicion that I've been set up.

That suspicion is confirmed two minutes later when a familiar voice calls out from the other side of the clearing, "Hello? Is someone there? They said I'd find the rest of the group up this way?"

I turn to see none other than Binx emerging from the trees, dressed in her tight black climbing pants and carrying a camping pack just like mine.

Chapter 7

BINX

I stop dead, my brain short-circuiting, stunned by the site of Seven alone in the clearing ahead of me.

It's like I conjured him there with the force of my rage.

He *blocked* me. Blocked me!

Me, the woman who he insists is such a child that she can't make an informed decision about who she wants to date. Meanwhile, instead of dealing with what happened between us yesterday, he's taken the path of maximum immaturity.

If someone had told me Seven would ghost me a few days ago, I would have laughed in their face and demanded they apologize. I never would have stood for that kind of disrespect toward my friend. Seven isn't a cowardly, selfish asshole. He wouldn't do that to anyone, especially not his best friend.

Those were *his* words, not mine. He called me his best friend while we were up that tree at my brother's wedding reception. Then, the very next evening, he was ready to pretend that I didn't exist.

A part of me wants to storm across the clearing and demand to know who the hell he thinks he is, but the other part is too worried about my free-falling stomach and the voice in my head warning that something is very wrong.

First of all, Seven shouldn't be here. I never mentioned this trip to him after our fight, and he wouldn't have signed up on his own. He loves rock-climbing, but he never takes off work, especially not for three whole days. And even if taking off work is part of his new ghosting, being-a-dick personality, he shouldn't be standing here all alone.

I'm half an hour late. Wendy Ann got stuck behind a garbage truck on the way to pick me up, and then the last road leading up to the meeting spot was washed out. Wendy Ann had to crawl up on top of her car to get cell service to text Lilac, then Lilac had to give us alternate directions, and then I had to strap on all my gear for the short hike up an access road not fit for my sister's little sedan.

Then, before I could set out, I had to endure a weirdly long hug from Wendy Ann.

A hug...

My sister isn't a hugger. She isn't much of a toucher, in general. Wendy Ann is a brain in a jar. She exists almost completely inside her own head.

But this morning, she hugged me and said that I could "totally survive for three days in the wilderness." At the time, I'd smiled at her worry wort side, and assured her that I absolutely could, and *would*, survive. I have tons of experience with backcountry camping, snacks in my pack to supplement the meals provided by the tour, and my water purifying supplies. I also have a tricked-out first aid kit and am an accomplished climber.

And while there might not be reliable cell service out here in the sticks, there surely will be where we're going. Even the Golden Spire bluffs are closer to civilization than the national forest outside Bad Dog.

I'm still not sure why we're meeting in the forest west of town to drive to a location two hours south*east* in Lilac's four-wheel drive vans, but that's part of the fun of a tour. You let someone else worry about the planning. All I have to do is throw my bag into the back of the van, pop my earbuds in, and settle in for the ride.

Or so I'd thought...

But there aren't any vans here, no tents to load up, not so much as a s'mores kit or a bottle of sunscreen.

There's just Seven, alone with his own bag, scowling at me like he's thinking about wringing my scrawny neck. Only my neck *isn't* scrawny, and I have no idea what he's so pissed about.

He's the one who's been acting like a spoiled teenager with zero conflict resolution skills.

"What?" I ask, propping my hands on my hips. "Why are you looking at me like that?"

"I can't believe you did this." His voice is a low, ominous rumble, like the thunder punctuating the air this morning.

Turns out, I was wrong about the weather holding. A storm to the south shifted course overnight and is set to

81

dump several inches of rain on us later this morning. But it's a fast-moving system and should clear out by the time we reach the bluffs.

The storm building inside of me, however...

"What are you talking about?" I ask, sharply. "You can't believe I did what? Signed up for the same climbing trip that you did? Believe me, if I'd known you were going to be here, I wouldn't have come."

That isn't true—I absolutely *would* have come; I've been dying for a face-to-face with him since my text messages started bouncing last night—but that doesn't matter.

What matters now, is showing him that he's being an idiot.

Throwing away our chance to be something more than friends is stupid, but throwing away our friendship? The best friendship of my entire life, and I would wager, his, too? Well, that's insanity, plain and simple. That's boss level dumb-dumb shit, and I'm not going to let him get away with it.

He's better than that. He's...the best.

I try to remember that as he huffs out a humorless laugh and shakes his head. "So, who helped you plan it? My mother? Sprout?" He curses beneath his breath as he begins to pace back and forth, his hiking boots silent on the pine needles. "I should have known. She was way too excited for a school day. All that grinning and dancing around the kitchen... But stupid me, I thought maybe the bullies had finally decided to take it easy on my kid."

My stomach tightens and my synapses fire, flinging

images of Wendy Ann and Sprout whispering together over wedding cake to the surface of my mind.

Then the two of them whispering over chips last night at the shower when Sprout's sitter dropped her off near the end of the party...

But no...

She wouldn't. My sister knows better than to collude with an eight-year-old in some kind of crazy Parent Trap scheme that isn't a Parent Trap scheme because Sprout isn't actually my child. But I know her better than a lot of moms know their kids, and I wouldn't put this past her for a second. She has her father's wild and stubborn streak, her grammy's meddling streak, and a drive to make her dreams come true that's going to serve her very well someday.

It might also, however, get her father and myself killed.

"Surviving for three days," I blurt out as I begin to pace the clearing, too.

Fuck, this is really happening. Wendy Ann did this. Maybe with Sprout, maybe alone, but either way she—

"No, it couldn't be alone," I mutter. "Or he wouldn't be here, too."

"What are you talking about?" Seven asks, his tone as exasperated as mine as I turn to shout, "You! You wouldn't be here if my sister had planned this alone. She had to have had help. Who dropped you off?"

His scowl fades as his eyes slowly widen. "My mother."

I pause, blinking in surprise. "Bettie? But she knows

better. She knows the woods can be dangerous, even for experienced outdoorspeople. She wouldn't put us in harm's way to play matchmaker. She just wouldn't."

"You really had nothing to do with this?" he asks in a softer voice.

I shake my head. "No! I didn't. I thought I was going on a climbing trip organized by Wendy Ann's friend Lilac."

"I did, too," he says. "My mom told me about it yesterday, a last-minute chance to get thirty percent off on a—"

"—a three-day Golden Spire bluffs excursion," I finish for him. "Yeah, I know. Same." I drop my head back with a sigh, watching the clouds swirl ominously above the trees. "I let Wendy Ann book it for me. I should have called Lilac myself. I should have known something wasn't right." I lift my chin, anger rising inside of me again as I pin Seven with a glare. "I probably would have if I hadn't been so distracted by my best friend *blocking* my texts like a huge, fucking asshole. What the hell was that about, Seven? Aren't you supposed to be the mature one? I mean, you're always acting like I'm too young to make adult decisions about my romantic life, but I've never ghosted someone because I was too chicken to have a conversation."

His scowl returns. "We don't have time for this right now. We have to make contact with someone back in town. Get them to pick us up before the storm breaks." He nods toward my pack. "But we'll have to use your phone. Mine seems to have mysteriously gone missing.

I'm guessing one of my double-crossing family members took it out while I was making coffee this morning."

My heart lurches. "We can't."

His scowl becomes a valley cutting through the middle of his forehead. "What do you mean *we can't*?"

"My cell fell in the toilet at the gas station about twenty miles back," I say. "Wendy Ann accidentally grabbed mine instead of hers on her way to the bathroom and dropped it in the toilet." He curses, and I wince. "Yeah, probably not an accident."

"*Obviously* not an accident. It was deliberate. They planned this. They wanted us out here alone with no way to call for help." He drags his hand through his hair, still damp from his morning shower.

And it's going to get damper very soon...

The sky rumbles again, the clearing dimming as the clouds thicken, darken.

I glance up, biting my lip. "Okay, first things first. We should put our rain gear on and look for shelter. Maybe there's something nearby, an old fire tower or abandoned ranger station. I know there used to be some out this way."

"There's nothing," he says, shrugging off his pack and pulling his rain shell from the side pocket. "I know this area. We're not far from the edge of my property, but until you reach my camp, there's nothing out here but trees."

I zip up my own shell, my heart lifting. "Oh, well, that's not so bad, then. At least they gave us a way out. We can just head to your camp."

"It's twenty miles east through dense forest," he

counters, his expression grim. "And once we get there, there's no landline to call for help."

My heart sinks again. "Shit."

"Yeah," he agrees.

"We'll be lucky to get through twenty miles of forest before dark. That's a big day on rough trails, even without rain making the ground soft."

"Yep," he says, his lips popping on the "p."

"And then it's at least another fifty miles back into town." My eyes narrow to slits as the urge to strangle my sister rises inside me. "We really *are* going to be stuck out here for three days. At least."

"We are," he says, his jaw clenching as he crouches to pull his rain guard over his pack. "And I only brought enough food for one."

I squat beside my pack, shifting my glare his way as I do the same. "Oh, and you don't plan to share? Is that what you're saying? You not only ghost your friends now, but you also starve them, too?"

"I didn't ghost you," he mutters, dropping his gaze to his bungee cords as he ties the rain guard down.

"Oh, no? Sure seemed like ghosting to me."

"I just needed a break, some time to think," he says.

"Then, you should have said that," I shoot back. "I'm not an asshole. I've always tried to be respectful of your boundaries. If you needed some time, all you had to do was ask for it."

"You know it isn't that simple," he mutters as he swings his pack onto his shoulders and turns to study the woods behind him.

"Why not?" I demand, struggling with my tangled

bungee cords as the wind starts to pick up. "Don't you feel like you can be honest with me? If so, that doesn't seem like a me problem, Seven. That seems like a—"

"Like a *me* problem?" He whirls on me, his eyes wide and wild. "Yeah, I know, Binx. It *is* a me problem. It's a me problem that I can't stop thinking about you, dreaming about you. It's a me problem that you're in my head all the fucking time and keeping my hands off you is becoming impossible. It's *my* fault that I wanted to snap Pierce in half for standing too close to you, let alone daring to put his fucking hand on your body. I get that. Believe me, I'm fully fucking aware."

I stand, gaping at him, my heart racing as another roll of thunder threatens to shake down the sky.

When it's quiet again, my lips part, but I don't know what to say, what to do. I only know that I don't want to scare him away, and he's clearly poised to bolt.

He was so scared of his feelings that he *ghosted* me, and that so isn't Seven.

Maybe that's why Bettie agreed to do this, because she knew it was the only way to keep her son from running away and ruining his second chance at love.

Love...

Seven might love me, too. Or at least want to touch me as desperately as I want to touch him.

Before I can fully assimilate the immensity of that, the sky opens up.

Hunching my shoulders against the stinging drops, I pull my hood up before hastily finishing securing the rain pouch onto my pack. By the time I stand, Seven is beside me, lifting my backpack into the air with one strong hand, holding it at shoulder height, so it's easier for me to slip on.

Once I've shrugged into the straps, I stare up at him. Rain streams into my face and creeps down into the neck of my shell as I stand there, desperately wanting to tell him that I feel the same way. I can't stop dreaming about him, either. In fact, sometime in the past year, he's become my biggest dream, even bigger than becoming a tattoo artist or competing on one of my favorite tattoo-themed reality shows someday.

That sure as hell scares *me*.

I've always been so independent. I changed my name when I was four years' old, for fuck's sake. I told my bossy, overbearing mother that I was "Binx" now, not Beatrice, and that I would no longer consent to wear clothes or go potty in the house until everyone in the family got on board. I don't remember exactly how it all went down, but according to family legend, I stayed outside playing in the mud in the nude for four hours until Mom finally relented and coaxed me into a bath.

That's who I am.

I'm a woman who is complete in myself, who knows my own mind, and who spent my childhood imagining I was the knight riding off on her horse to slay the dragon, not the princess waiting in her tower to be rescued. The idea that a man has become so central to my happiness is terrifying.

But it's also beautiful. When I look at Seven, when our eyes meet, I *know* this is where I belong—with him, by his side, taking on the world together. There's no doubt in my mind about that.

Now, I guess I have three days to make sure that, by the time we leave the forest, there's no doubt in his, either.

SEVEN

I've never been so grateful for rain stinging into my face and wind whipping around my ears. In the chaos of the storm, conversation is impossible.

Which is good.

I can't talk to Binx right now, or I'll say something else I shouldn't, something that will dig this hole even deeper.

I shouldn't have said any of the things I confessed to in the clearing. Nothing good will come from Binx knowing the way I really feel. There's no way forward for us down that road. The only way to keep her in my life long term, is to snuff out the attraction I feel for her and bury it six feet under.

I can do that.

I *have* to do it, for Sprout if not for myself.

My little girl adores this woman. She needs Binx in her life as much as she needs her family. If I'm the reason she loses a friend who's been such a source of comfort and support for her, the guilt will eat me alive. I don't want to be that kind of parent, the selfish kind who doesn't think about all the ways my actions affect my child.

I just need some time away from Binx, time to get my head on straight and distract my dick with a more age-appropriate woman.

And yes, she's right, I should have *asked* for the time, not blocked her calls like a coward. But last night, I was too close to the edge to make rational decisions. I knew if I read one more text, I'd be on my way to her place to ruin our friendship forever.

If we sleep together, it's over. I know that deep in my bones. I'm not the kind of man who easily transitions from lovers to friends. I've only tried it a few times, and it's never gone well, not even with women I was casually dating.

There's nothing casual about what I feel for Binx.

When I realized we were trapped out here, I was angry, sure, but only because I was concerned for her well-being. What if I don't have enough food to get us through the next few days? What if she gets hurt on the trail, and I can't get her to medical attention in time? Being able to protect the people I love is top priority for me, and anything that threatens that, drives me out of my fucking mind.

Then, once I realized she had nothing to do with getting us stuck in the middle of nowhere, the guilt hit full force.

If something happens to Binx because my mother and daughter are maniacs who have watched too many Hallmark romance movies, I'll never forgive myself. She's too precious to put at risk for any reason, but especially for a chance at happily ever after with me.

It would be more like happily *never* after—my relationship with my first wife taught me that. I loved Millie with an obsession that probably wasn't healthy, yes, but that didn't mean I knew how to give her what she needed.

She asked me a hundred times to take time off, to prioritize "quality time" with her and Sprout, but I couldn't...especially back then. Millie couldn't find work after Sprout was born and money was tight. Yes, we still had a little leftover at the end of each month, but not much, and our savings was a joke. All it would have taken was one illness or injury at work to lose the safety I'd worked so hard for.

So, I tripled down on building our wealth, trusting that Millie would eventually see that providing for her and Sprout was one of the big ways I showed my love.

She didn't...

She didn't, and it eventually destroyed us. But even if I had realized that I was losing her before it was too late, I don't know if it would have made a difference.

For better or worse, this is the way I'm built.

I grew up feeling like the rug was about to be ripped out from under my feet at any moment. Mom worked her fingers to the bone to provide for my brothers and me, but when we were younger, we struggled. A lot. When my father pulled his head out of his ass and pitched in, we had reliable food and shelter, but when he got swept up in one of his get-rich-quick schemes or hit the road with his dirt-biking buddies for weeks at a time, we skated perilously close to the edge.

I remember nights going to bed hungry and mornings hiding from the bill collectors pounding on the door. If one of my mom's friends hadn't stepped in at the last minute to help us cover the mortgage when I was in fifth grade, we would have been out on the street in the middle of winter.

I swore back then, when I was still just a kid washing dishes at a diner after school for two bucks an hour, that I would never fail my family the way my father had failed his.

I would provide for the people I loved, no matter what.

If my high school friends had *asked* me about robbing the pawn shop that night, instead of tricking me into driving the getaway car without warning, I might have actually agreed to it. Mr. Albert, the owner of the shop, leered at my mother's cleavage every time she went in to pawn one of her few valuable possessions to keep the lights on or buy my little brother a cheap pair of snow boots. He seemed to get off on her shame. I'd fantasized about punching him in his skeezy face since I was about twelve years old.

I might have willingly signed on to steal a little extra safety for my family from that asshole, and I sure as hell would have planned a better heist than my idiot friends.

That's why I didn't bother appealing my conviction, even though my lawyer thought I had a decent chance at having my sentence reversed. He believed that I was an innocent victim who was just at the wrong place at the wrong time, and that was partly true. But if I'd been given the chance to make the right decision, I'm not sure I would have. In my mind, I deserved to serve my time.

Ensuring the people I love were taken care of was *that* important to me. As a dumb kid, I might have risked going to prison for it. As an adult, I work like an animal for it. And when I was first married, building my nest egg for the future came before anything else.

I would rather my mom be mad at me for missing the family Christmas party than lose the money I made taking a group of hunters out for deer season that Saturday. I would rather leave my wife lonely every night while I snagged an evening shift at the lumber yard than stay home and try to save our marriage. The fear of not having enough set aside to keep my people safe was too strong to do anything else.

Then the car wreck turned my world upside down and money was more important than ever. I needed money to pay for Sprout's hospital bills, her physical therapy...and to put a deposit down on my wife's headstone. Millie and I had been separated for three months by then, but until that night, I'd still had hope that we would work it out.

After the accident, I grieved her all the more intensely, knowing she died disappointed in me and the love I'd tried to give her.

My love wasn't enough. *I* wasn't enough, and I'm not sure I ever will be, not for anyone who wants a "normal" relationship, anyway.

That's why it's better for me to spend my time with someone like Pammy, an older woman who has been through enough shit in her own life to be happy with a low-key, friends-with-benefits situation. We can have fun and support each other as friends without romance getting in the way. We'll enjoy our connection for as long as things are good, then part ways without drama or pain.

I've had enough drama and pain to last two lifetimes.

The thought is barely through my head when Binx cries out behind me. I turn in time to see the edge of the deer trail we've been following give way beneath her.

One second, she's close enough to reach out and touch. The next, she's sliding down the side of the embankment, followed by a rush of mud and a small tree that's been uprooted by the sudden violence of the storm.

On instinct, I lunge for her, but it's already too late.

She's gone.

Chapter 9

BINX

I'm wearing my grippiest hiking boots, the ones that have saved me on more slippery rock faces than I can count, but it's not enough. I dig my heels into the soaked ground beneath me, scrambling to gain traction, but my shoes only glide across the slick mud as I zip down the hill, faster and faster.

I throw out my arms, trying to find something to hold onto, but the plants I manage to grasp slide through my wet fingers or are instantly uprooted by the force of my momentum.

I'm really moving now, careening down the mountainside with a speed that would be exhilarating if I didn't know it's only a matter of time before I run into a tree or tumble off a ledge. I don't know this area well enough to be sure, but it looks like there's a drop off ahead. How big a drop off, I have no idea, but I don't want to find out at twenty miles per hour.

A fresh rush of adrenaline dumping into my bloodstream, I roll over onto my side and then my stomach, wincing as my hip skims over a rock. But better bruised than broken beyond repair, and I'll have a better chance at holding onto something if I'm using both hands.

I try clawing my fingers into the mud but realize almost instantly that that's a losing game. The sudden downpour has made the top level of soil unstable. I throw out my right arm to catch the trunk of a tree, instead, but am quickly knocked loose as a smaller, uprooted tree, tumbling down the hill behind me, collides with my shoulder.

I curse and sputter, flailing my arms as I try to free myself from the tangle of limbs, but it's no use. I'm trapped.

And then, I'm out of the mud.

I hit open air and time slows for a horrible, gut-wrenching second, electrifying every nerve in my body. Then, before I can brace myself, before I can do anything except utter a string of mental obscenities that are a sorry excuse for "last words," I'm falling.

Thank God, I don't fall far, but it's still terrifying.

I hit the ground with a cry of pain, my breath rushing out of my lungs with enough force to leave me paralyzed.

I'm still on the ground, clutching at my chest beneath the limbs, fighting to suck in oxygen and assess my injuries at the same time, when suddenly Seven is there. He lifts the tree off me and tosses it aside like it weighs nothing at all, his soaked hair flying around his face as he moves.

For a moment, as I lie there in the mud, looking up at him, I can't help but think how fucking gorgeous he is when he's filthy and worried about me. But soon, the fact that I can't breathe becomes my one and only concern.

I roll onto my side, attempting to struggle out of my pack—thinking that maybe getting the straps off will help —but it's like my chest is caving in. My shoulders curl forward, no matter how hard I try to roll them back, and my fingers are going numb.

"Lie still. I've got you." Seven crouches beside me, quickly freeing the clasp holding my straps together across the top of my chest.

In seconds he has my pack off and is running gentle hands over my neck and ribs to check for broken bones. I try to tell him that I'm okay—I just can't breathe—but oxygen is required for speaking, as well.

All I can do is wheeze and panic in earnest as my brain begins to ache in my skull and the next inhalation refuses to come.

"In your belly, baby," he says. "Breathe into your belly."

He shifts on top of me, guiding my arms up over my head. Pinning both my wrists to the ground with one hand, he brings the other to press lightly against my stomach, just below my ribs.

"Right here," he says, his worried gaze locked on mine as he gives my belly a gentle shake. "Breathe into my palm. Drop your diaphragm and fill your stomach with air."

I try, I really do, but my ribs remain locked and the panic is becoming overwhelming. Silent tears stream down my face as my heart threatens to pound through my ribs, and for a moment, I'm certain I'm going to die.

I'm going to die from getting the wind knocked out

of me. I'll be a sad punchline in some medical journal somewhere, like those people who died from hiccups, and my family will never live it down. My mother will have yet another reason to be upset about my weirdness, her black sheep of a daughter who couldn't even die in a normal way, and Wendy Ann will never forgive herself for her disastrous attempt at playing matchmaker.

Black fuzz creeps in around the edges of my vision and my arms go numb. I realize I'm losing consciousness, but before my eyes can slide closed, Seven's face is inches from mine, whispering, "Breathe, Binx McGuire. You fucking breathe for me, baby. Right now. That's an order."

Then, he kisses me—*really* kisses me. His lips press against mine, firm and demanding, laying claim to my mouth with an intensity that sends a wave of shock zipping through me from head to toe.

Thank God, the shock wave is enough to set my body free. The vice around my ribs loosens with a spasm. I gasp in a breath, filling the hand Seven still presses to my stomach and then some.

I pant against his lips as he murmurs, "That's it, there you go. You're okay. You're okay now, baby, I promise."

He releases my wrists and starts to shift away, but I move faster. I curl my fingers around his neck, dragging him back into my arms, and for once, he doesn't fight me.

He comes to me with a groan, kissing me even harder this time, his tongue stroking into my mouth and his hands suddenly everywhere. His touch is still gentle, concerned, but I can feel the hunger there, too.

This isn't just fear, this is longing, passion.

He has to feel it, too. He just has to.

I wrap my legs around his hips and flex my muscles, drawing him closer, my hope bolstered by the rock-hard length behind his fly. I moan and lift my hips, thrilling to the feel of him pulsing against me through our clothes.

He wants me, he really does. He wants me and he's finally done fighting it.

He grinds between my legs, making my breath rush out against his lips as we continue to kiss like we're never going to get enough. I know I never will. Kissing him is even better than I imagined it would be. It's the best thing I've ever felt, even while lying in cold mud that smells vaguely of earthworms.

"Fuck, Binx," he rumbles against my lips in between frantic, hungry kisses. "You feel so fucking good."

"I want you so much," I say, shuddering as he continues to fuck me through our clothes. I haven't made out like this since high school, but it's indescribably hot. It doesn't matter that we're both still fully dressed and covered in mud and soaked to the skin, I can't remember the last time I was this happy.

This relieved...

This is all I've wanted for so long. Just the chance to be this close to him, to show him how much he means to me.

"You're the only one," I continue, arching into his touch as he cups my breast though my shirt, squeezing tight enough to send another jolt of arousal rocketing straight to my core. "I don't want anyone else. I'll never want anyone else. It's just you, Seven. Just you."

He stiffens against me, and I instantly know I've said too much.

"No," I insist, gripping the front of his shirt as he tries to pull away. "No, you can't run away from me. Not now. Not when we're so close."

"We have to get back to the trail," he says, his gaze on my shoulder, as if looking me in the eye is suddenly too much for him.

"No," I insist, emotion making my chest tight again. "We don't. We have to be honest with each other. This is more than attraction. This is something special. You're my best friend, Seven. I love you." He winces, but I force myself to keep going. "And you love me. And yes, it's a friendly kind of love now, but it could be so much more. For both of us. You know it could. You *know*. So, please, stop pushing me away. I can't take it anymore. It's killing me."

His wince becomes an expression of such exquisite pain that I wish I could turn back time and shove the stupid words back in my stupid mouth.

I know all about his wife. I know how she died, and I've heard enough from Bettie to know that it ripped Seven apart. He never fully recovered from the loss. The fact that they were separated when the crash happened piled another layer of guilt and misery onto an already tragic situation. Afterwards, he crawled into an emotional cave, rolled a rock in front of the entrance, and refused to come out for anyone.

Even Sprout doesn't get the full force of his love.

I feel it when they're together, how desperate she is to break through that final wall to the tender-hearted man inside. On an intellectual level, she knows her daddy loves her more than anything in the world, but there's a part of her that wants more.

More of his time, more of his goofy smiles, more of the relaxed, easy-loving man I've only seen a few times, when the stars aligned to make him feel safe enough to come out of the prison he locked himself away in when his marriage ended in tragedy.

"I'm sorry," I whisper, touching soft fingertips to his face.

"Don't be," he says in a rough voice. "This is my fault. All of it. I'm the one who should be sorry. I was trying to be better, to handle this the right way for you and me and Sprout, but..." He shifts his tortured gaze my way. "I can't. I'm not strong enough. And I'm..." He swallows, his throat working. "Your mother was right to look at me the way she did yesterday. Nothing good will come of this. Of you and me. That's why there can't *be* a you and me."

Tears spring into my eyes. "No, you don't get to make that decision, not without me. What about that kiss, Seven? Are you just going to ignore how right that felt? How perfect?" I fight to keep my voice from wobbling as I add, "Kisses like that don't happen every day."

He sits back on his heels with his head bowed and his hands fisted in his lap. He looks like a penitent in front of some primal god, one who demands his worshippers show up covered in mud and pain.

This is hurting him, too. He's hurting us both so much, and for what?

Why?

This is obviously about more than the age gap. But before I can try to get through to him again, another uprooted tree slides down the embankment. The rain is slowing, and the tree isn't moving fast enough to do either of us any damage, but it's enough to put the moment behind us as Seven grabs our packs, and I haul myself to my feet, hobbling after him toward a pond not far away.

By the time we've cleaned the mud off our clothes as best we can with leaves and silty water, Seven's walls are up again. Gone is the man who looked at me like it was killing him not to hold me. In his place is the man people meet at the bar when he's standing in for Bettie's usual bouncer on summer concert nights.

He looks hard, unreachable, even a little dangerous...

But I'm not scared. I never have been, and I never will be. Seven isn't a danger to good people.

At least, not to anyone but himself.

Is that the real reason he's fought this thing between us tooth and nail? Because he doesn't think he's good enough for me? Because he thinks my mother was right to look at him like a wad of gum stuck to her shoe?

If so, that's...insane.

And heartbreaking.

Because this man silently shrugging both our packs onto his back and shifting the straps until he's managed to take on the load of two people without a second of hesitation, is so much better than "good enough." He's a devoted father who would do anything for his baby girl. He's a son who's always there for his mother, and a brother who drops anything to help when Nolan's old

Mustang is on the fritz or Greer needs an extra pair of hands to finish a roof installation on schedule.

He's the hardest worker I know, driven as hell, and excels at anything he puts his mind to. He's also the kind of friend who brings chicken soup and ginger ale when you're sick, supports your dreams like they're his own, and can't rest until he knows the people he cares about are safe in their beds after a night on the town.

I live for his "Home safe yet, Trouble?" texts.

Maybe it's crazy, but those four little words make me feel more loved than soliloquies from men I've dated before.

Seven is twice the man they were and so much better than "good enough," but now isn't the time to try to convince him of that. Now is the time to get moving before we lose anymore daylight.

"I can carry my pack," I say, doing my best to hide the hitch in my step as we follow the curve of the pond around to an easier route up to the top of the ridge.

"No, you can't," he says, his words as distant as his expression. "You're favoring your hip."

"It's just bruised, not broken or sprained. I just need to walk it off. I can—"

"No," he cuts in again without so much as a glance my way. "If you add weight to it, you could make it worse, and you unable to walk is the last thing I need. Two packs, I can handle. I can't carry you and our supplies, and there's nothing at the camp. I'm planning to stock some canned goods for the winter, but I was waiting until the kitchen renovation was done in the cabin. There might be a bag of marshmallows and chocolate from the last time Sprout and I made s'mores, but that's it, and we can't survive on that for three days."

Survive...

The word gives me pause, and I fall silent as we start up the hill.

Is he really worried about survival? I mean, I'm not injured *that* badly, and he could always come back for our packs if I were. But then, what if he couldn't find the bags again later? Or what if animals dragged them off to tear at the fabric until they got to the food inside? I guess it isn't crazy to think that if we're not careful, things could go downhill pretty fast.

It also isn't crazy to see why Seven always jumps to "worst-case scenario" thinking. He's lived through a lot of worst-case scenarios in his life, from his family almost losing their house as a kid, to Bettie's traumatic divorce from his father, to ending up in prison for a crime he didn't even commit, to his separation from his wife ending in her death and a traumatic injury to his daughter.

He hasn't had a lot of experience with "easy" or even uncomplicated.

But I know it could be easy for us, that kiss proved it beyond the shadow of a doubt. That was the kind of kiss people write songs about, the kind you can't believe is real until you're lucky enough to experience one in real life.

Now that I have, I'm even more determined to fight for this, for *us*.

He can push me away for now, but if he thinks I'll give up because he's thrown up a wall, he's got another think coming. I'm a rock climber. I can handle walls, and once we're safe at his camp, I intend to put all my skills to use scaling Seven's.

We *are* going to make it there safely. Fate can be a bitch, but not even the cruelest twist of her knife would give two people a kiss like that, then take them out before they could do more. I'm going to feel Seven against me again—properly, this time, with clean bodies in a clean bed—or I'm not the girl who named herself when she was just a kid.

He's stubborn, but I'm *way* worse, and now that I have real evidence that he wants me too?

Well, he hasn't seen anyone dig their heels in the way I'm about to dig in mine.

He thinks he's seen obstinate from me, but he hasn't seen anything yet.

Chapter 10

SEVEN

As morning becomes afternoon and the weight of carrying two packs starts to wear on me, I focus on the tension in my shoulders and the ache in my back. I focus on the way my damp hiking pants chafe at the waist and the repulsive feel of tacky boxer briefs clinging to my balls—anything to keep my mind off dry humping Binx in the mud.

But fuck...even physically miserable and hating myself for crossing that line, I can't completely banish the memory. I can still feel the heat of her lips on mine, and every time I glance back to make sure she's still behind me on the deer trail, meeting her gaze for a split second is enough to make me ache.

I want to hold her again, kiss her again. I want to forget all the reasons we can't be together and lose myself in her beautiful body. I want to wrap myself in the sweet strength of this incredible woman and let her convince me that I'm the man for her.

Even though I know that's not true.

I might be what she *wants* right now, but that wouldn't last, and I'm sure as hell not what she needs.

I prove that by being a grouchy asshole when she asks to stop a little too soon after our last water break, only relenting when she asks if I would prefer that she pee her pants as we walk.

"Not particularly," I say, swaying to a stop with a sigh.

"Then, I'm allowed to take a bathroom break?"

"Knock yourself out." I shift to lean my back against the thick trunk of a tree behind me, letting it take some of the weight off my shoulders. In return, it sends a sprinkle of raindrops down on my head. It stopped raining several hours ago, but the fall leaves are holding on to enough moisture that we'll be dribbled on as long as we're in the woods today.

And we're going to be in the woods for at least a couple more hours. Between Binx's injury and me being weighed down by two packs, we'll be lucky to make it to my camp before nightfall, and that's if nothing else goes wrong.

Binx pauses on her way off the deer path, arching a brow my way. "Don't you want to take the packs off for a few minutes? Take a rest?"

I shake my head and fold my arms over my chest. "I don't want to waste time getting them back on. We have to keep moving."

"I know, I know," she says, with a subtle roll of her eyes. "I'll pee as quickly as I can, I promise."

"Good," I grunt, hating myself for being an asshole, but a little proud of it, too. I should show her this side of myself more often. If she saw what a grumpy fucker I can be, she would realize I'm more trouble than I'm worth.

Muttering something beneath her breath that I can't quite make out, she disappears behind a fallen log not far from the trail. I cast my gaze toward the ridgeline, giving her privacy. After her tumble down the mountain, we moved farther away from the edge of the incline, but not too far, since it's the easiest way to be sure we're staying on the right track. The ridge tracks due east, where it hooks up with the ridge on my own property.

I'm pretty sure we passed the property line for my camp about a mile back, but there's a chance we're still a little farther out.

I haven't been to this side of the camp often—I've been too busy working on the infrastructure on the other side—but I remember thinking it would be a good place to teach bouldering classes down the road. The rocks around here aren't tall enough for proper climbing, but there's a lot of fun to be had with smaller rock formations, a bag of chalk, and some crash pads.

Though nothing about that sounds like fun right now.

My shoulders are on fire. I work out like a beast, but even my impressive shoulder press hasn't prepared me for the awkward way I'm carrying this weight.

I'm considering strapping one bag to my front, while keeping the other on my back—even though it will be hard to see over the top of the tall pack—when Binx reappears.

She's wincing and walking a bit more gingerly than before, but when I ask her about it, she snaps, "I'm fine,

Seven. I'm not made of glass, I promise. And I can carry my pack now. My hip isn't sore at all anymore."

I don't dignify that with an answer. I just turn and continue moving east along the faint deer trail, slowing my pace slightly to accommodate for her ginger gait, which only gets worse as the miles pass. By the time we've reached a part of the land I definitely recognize from my four-wheeler treks with Sprout, her brow is locked in a furrow of pain.

"I have ibuprofen in my bag," I offer.

"I'm fine," she says in a strained voice, wincing again as she steps over a rock in the path.

"You look fine," I say dryly. "What with all the wincing and limping."

She glares my way. "Okay, Sarcasm Man, I'm not fine, but it's nothing an ibuprofen is going to help."

I return her scowl. "Then what is it?"

She averts her gaze, muttering, "Nothing. It's fine. I'll be fine. We're almost there."

"We're not," I correct her, not in the business of peddling pretty lies. "We have at least two miles left, maybe three."

"That's fine," she insists. "I can make it two miles. I have to make it. Like you said, you can't carry me."

"Is it your hip? Are you—"

She sighs. "No, Seven, it isn't my hip."

"Then what—"

"It's chafing, okay?" she cuts in, with a mixture of annoyance and what sounds like embarrassment, though I can't say for sure. I've never heard Binx embarrassed.

"Chafing? Where?"

She winces again. "My inner thighs. These pants are fine when they're dry, but when they're soaking wet...not so much."

"Why didn't you say something before?" I ask, grinding to a halt. "I have Band-Aids in my pack."

"Yeah, so do I," she says, "but I didn't want to slow us down. Your head almost exploded when I asked to stop to pee."

"It didn't almost explode. I was just worried about losing the light before we made it to camp." I pop the clasp on the straps holding both packs around my waist, letting them slide to the ground. "But chafing is serious. It could get infected or bad enough that you won't be able to get back on the trail tomorrow."

"God forbid," she mutters, but she obediently shuffles over to me when I point to the ground beside the pack. "You know, we could just wait it out at the camp. If they don't hear from us for a few days, they'll come looking. They might even come sooner. Wendy Ann is my most logical sibling. Sooner or later, she's going to realize she did a dumb, illogical thing and want to make it right."

"I'm not going to hold my breath," I say, locating my first aid kit and setting it on top of Binx's closed pack. I pop it open, sifting through the various sized bandages as I add as nonchalantly as possible, "Drop your drawers. Let's see what we're dealing with."

"I can do it myself," she says, holding out her hand. "In private."

"I'm sure you can, but it'll be easier to get the wounds cleaned and the bandages in the right position with help.

We need to get this right the first time. I only have enough supplies to last for a few days."

Her head falls back with a sigh, but she grumbles a surly, "Fine," and reaches for the button on her pants. "But you can't judge my disgusting underwear. I swear, they were clean before I fell down a hill and rolled around in the mud."

"Not something I'm worried about right now," I say, keeping my expression impassive as she drags her zipper down and gingerly guides her pants around her knees.

I will not let her see that the sight of her in underwear —even modest underwear grimy with mud stains—does things to me. She's just so beautiful, so perfect, so...Binx.

She's also hurt...

I curse beneath my breath, my awareness of everything but her pain fading as I see the raw, savaged flesh on her inner thighs.

"It's not that bad," she says in a tight voice, her breath hissing out as I gently grip the skin beneath the wound on her left side. "Don't touch it."

"I'm not touching it," I murmur. "I'm just trying to see how far back it goes."

"Far," she says, "it goes back far. I said, don't touch it."

"I'm not, baby, I promise," I say, the word out of my mouth before I can think better of it. I glance up quickly, hoping maybe Binx didn't notice, but her expression makes it clear I didn't get so lucky.

She looks...stricken, like my words are salt in her wound.

"I'm sorry," I say, feeling like an absolute piece of shit.

I promised myself after the idiotic way I behaved in the mud that I'd get control of myself. "Bad habit. The only person I'm used to comforting when they're hurt is Sprout and...she's my baby."

"She is," Binx agrees with a sad little nod that does nothing to banish the shame worming through my chest. "It's fine. I know you don't mean it."

But I do mean it. I mean it with everything in me. But at least I have the self-control not to say *that* part out loud.

"This is bad, Binx," I say instead, chewing on my bottom lip for a second. "We need to get it clean, but I'm hesitant to use the alcohol swab. I think we'd be better off with plain old soap and warm water for this."

"But we can't get to soap and warm water, right?" she asks.

"There's soap at the cabin, but no warm water. I haven't had the chance to replace the old hot water heater, and we're still another hour or so away. I'd prefer to get this clean now, before I bandage it."

She nods. "Yeah, me, too. I don't want any infectious critters trapped under my bandage. Just give me the alcohol swab, I can clean it."

I arch a dubious brow. "Are you sure? It always hurts more to hurt yourself. I had to stich up a gash in my leg one time, when I took a fall off a cliff and was too far from civilization to get to the ER in time. It was fucking miserable."

She winces. "Ow. That sounds horrific. Did you cry?"

"Yeah," I say. "And I almost passed out. Twice."

"Shit." She wrinkles her nose. "I mean, this obviously isn't as bad as a wound like that, but—"

"It's pretty bad," I cut in, exhaling as I glance down at the twin red wounds on either side of her thighs. They're oozing a bit of blood and look bruised in the middle. "I'm no doctor, but they look like third-or-fourth-degree abrasions. I can't believe you kept walking all this time without stopping me sooner." Another wave of shame curdles my stomach. "I'm sorry I made you feel like you couldn't ask for a break."

"No, it isn't your fault," she says, her tone softer than it's been in hours. "It's mine. I felt stupid. I know these pants are a little too tight and hold water for way too long, but I wore them anyway. I thought it would be okay, since the rain was supposed to pass, and I was going to be in a van all morning. Then, once I realized how bad it was, I was kind of afraid to look. I mean, it's not like I can stop walking. We have to get to the cabin. The only thing worse than sleeping in a cabin with no way to call for help is sleeping out in the middle of the woods with no way to call for help."

I give her leg a gentle squeeze, right below the knee. "Pride's a bitch."

Her lips twitch up. "Yeah, it is."

"I know, I've been there," I say. "But we'll get this bandaged up and you can borrow something to wear. I brought an extra pair of pants. I usually don't for climbing trips, but since I ripped the ass out of a pair on our last climbing trip, I figured, I should have a backup."

Her smile widens. "I'll never forget those black pants giving way to rainbow unicorn boxer briefs."

"They were a—"

"Gift from Sprout," she finishes for me with a soft laugh. "I know, I know. But it was still funny. It's sweet that you actually wear them. Most dads wouldn't."

"I'm not most dads," I say, letting the words serve as a reminder of the kind of man I want to be—the kind who doesn't get his daughter's hopes up about a relationship that's never going to happen.

And the type who doesn't ground her for the next decade for pulling a stunt like this. After all, as long as Binx and I both get out of here in one piece, without any irreversible mistakes being made, it'll all be okay.

Though, speaking of irreversible mistakes...

"These might scar," I tell her as I clean my hands as best I can with one alcohol wipe. "Hopefully they'll stop bleeding and scab over once the irritation stops, but the wounds are deep."

"I think it will be okay," she says, a mixture of hope and concern in her voice. "I chafed pretty badly with these pants once before, and it healed faster than I could have imagined." She sucks in a breath and sets her jaw. "I'm going to be fine. And I'm ready. Just...do it. Fast. Like a shot."

"All right," I say, bracing myself to hurt her. Even knowing I'm helping with the hurt, it's not going to be easy. "Here we go."

I dab the wipe over the wound on her right thigh, the worse of the two. Her muscles go rigid beneath my other hand, but she doesn't make a sound aside from a sharp hiss of breath. I keep going, cleaning the wound thoroughly.

By the time I'm done, she's trembling all over.

"Okay?" I ask.

"Just hurry," she says in a breathy voice. "It's bad, but it'll be over soon."

"It will be," I promise, pulling out another clean wipe and giving her other wound the same treatment, "There, all done, the worst part is over. We just need to give the skin around them a second to dry before I put on the bandages." I lift my gaze. "How you holding up?"

She looks down, her pale features weary. "Okay." She slides her tongue across her bottom lip. "Are you intimidated?"

"By what?"

"By my badass pain tolerance."

I smile. "Oh, yeah. For sure. Totally intimidated, but not surprised. You're way more badass than I am."

"Thanks," she says, her lips hooking up on one side. "Pretty lies make a girl feel good while she's waiting to pull up her pants. The petting is nice, too."

I'm about to ask what she means by that, then realize I've been absentmindedly stroking her thighs beneath her wounds, running my thumbs up and down her velvety soft skin.

I pull my hands away with a self-conscious laugh. "Sorry."

"Don't be," she murmurs. "It was nice. Your touch is...nice."

I hold her gaze and for a moment as I imagine stripping her panties down to her ankles and showing her how nice I can be. I want my mouth between her legs, kissing her in the most intimate way a man can kiss a woman. I want to devour her, worship her, make her tremble for reasons that have nothing to do with pain.

Then, I want to take her from behind, slow and careful, so as not to cause her anything but pleasure.

And I swear, Binx can read my mind. She bites her bottom lip and gives a slight nod, as if giving me permission to ravage her right here in the middle of the woods.

But I don't.

I carefully apply the bandages, fetch my spare pants from my bag, and turn my back as she puts them on. Then, I swing both bags back onto my back again and set off at a slower pace, willing myself to take it easy, even though I'm desperate to get to the bathroom at the cabin.

A cold shower is exactly what the doctor ordered to cool things off between us.

Or, worst-case scenario, I can jerk off in the shower, hopefully taking the edge off enough that we can make it through a night in close quarters without doing anything we'll regret.

Yeah, good luck with that, buddy, my dick says a mile later, from where he's still rock hard and aching behind my fly.

This isn't going to be easy, but important things rarely are.

It's important that I never cross the line with Binx again. That's the right thing to do, and I'm going to keep fighting for the right, even if a part of me is certain it's a battle I'm doomed to lose.

Chapter 11

BINX

Our progress slows even more after our first aid session. I'm swimming in Seven's pants, holding them up with one hand as I scuttle forward, doing my best not to disturb the bandages underneath.

The slower pace adds to the anxiety of watching the last sliver of sun sink behind the trees. There's still a dusky glow in the air, but the temperature starts dropping fast. Soon, my fleece and rain shell don't feel like they're providing enough warmth, but there's no way I'm asking to stop to grab my puffer vest from my pack.

Seven wouldn't want me to be cold, but he's already suffering. He's the strongest man I know, but after a full day of carrying double gear, I can tell he's about to reach his limit. When we stopped to grab granola bars half an hour ago, he groaned as he loaded the second pack onto his back.

Seven never groans. He never complains or shows any

sign of weakness, and I hate that he's starting to break because of me.

I want to break through his defenses; I don't want to break the man himself.

I promise myself I'll find some way to help him feel better as soon as we get to the cabin. I think I threw my stickable pain strips into my bag last night, just in case my lower back started acting up. I can offer to stick them where it hurts for him.

Buoyed by the thought, I waddle a little faster, counting my steps the way I used to do as a kid when forced out of our cozy house to hike with my family. I hated hiking back then—probably because I was one of the youngest, and the older kids never slowed their pace for me or Wendy Ann. Every time I was forced out into the woods, I would make up games to help the time go by faster.

If I counted to one thousand in my head without missing a number or saying anything aloud to my siblings, the hike would be over by the time I reached one thousand one. Or, if I walked backwards for one hundred steps, then forward, then backwards again, then skipped sideways, I'd find a shortcut and be able to sit on a bench and wait for everyone else to catch up.

I never "won" these games, but they served their purpose. They kept my mind from fixating on my discomfort.

Now, I'm up to six hundred and twenty-seven steps on my third count to one thousand, when Seven glances over his shoulder with a relieved smile. "We're here. The cabin's just over that ridge."

I practically sag to the ground with relief. "Oh, thank God. I'm so tired. I didn't want to admit it until I knew we'd made it, but I think I could sleep for a thousand years. And eat an entire buffet all by myself. But since food is in short supply, I'll settle for the sleeping."

"Same," Seven says, starting forward with a bit more spring in his step, me finally beside him on the trail now that it's wide enough for two. "Though I was thinking, I'd love a hot bath first, if you'd like one, too. If we can get a fire going, I might have enough pots and pans to heat up water for the old tub on the porch."

I frown up at him. "On the porch?"

"The former owner, the one who bought it from the Boy Scouts originally, liked to bathe outside. Apparently, she was a bath influencer."

I laugh. "A bath influencer? As in she...influenced people to bathe regularly? Is that really something we need persuasion from strangers on the internet to do?"

"I think she convinced people to take pretty baths? Or something?" He shakes his head, looking so adorably confused that I want to kiss him again. But that's nothing new. I've wanted to kiss him again all day, even when he was being a big old grouch. "I don't know," he continues, "but there's a giant, clawfoot tub on the back porch. Sprout went 'swimming' in it a few times before the weather got too cold. She thinks we should leave it there, but I don't think a fancy bath is going to match the rustic design we're going with for the rest of the buildings."

I shrug. "Who cares? It sounds cool. Better to have cool quirky things than matching things."

He makes a doubtful sound. "I don't know. I don't

want to scare people away by being *too* quirky, and you can see the back of the cabin from several of the guest cottages."

"How are bookings so far?" I ask. "You opened the website for reservations, right?"

He nods, some of the weariness fading from his expression. "Yeah, I already have three bookings for corporate retreats next summer. They booked the entire camp with the bonus adventure package."

"That's amazing! Congrats."

He fights a grin. "Thanks, but don't get too excited. I have to sell at least four more to break even for the year. Even with keeping most of the building and renovation in the family, this hasn't been cheap."

"But it's smart. You're building a business that's going to be profitable for years to come. Once the initial investment is over, you'll have a cash cow on your hands."

"I hope so," he says, "but don't jinx it. This is Sprout's college fund. The adventure tours pay for everything we need, but this is going to take my ability to save to the next level. I'm hoping to have enough stashed away that she won't have to take out a single loan."

"That's smart. My loans are a pain in my ass, and I won't even be using my degree once I start tattooing." I smile. "You're a good dad. Sprout's lucky to have you."

He grunts, his smile fading. "I try."

"You succeed."

He presses his lips together, his brow furrowing. For a moment, I think he's going to argue with me, but then the cabin appears over the next rise, and he heaves a giant sigh of relief. "Fuck. I've never been so happy to see this place."

I echo his sigh, relief making my knees wobbly. "Me, too. I would race you to the porch, but I'm injured and your spine is probably never going to be the same again as it is."

He laughs. "My spine is fine, but that bath is sounding better and better. There's the tub. Fancy, right?"

I glance in the direction of his nod, spotting a dark green clawfoot tub that blends in with the peeling green paint on the porch. But it's white on the inside and looks gorgeous. "I bet that bath lady sold a lot of bath bombs. Or salts or soap or whatever she was peddling on social media."

"Bath potions," he says. "That's what Sprout told me, anyway. She looked the woman up online. She's now moved into a bigger, nicer cabin, with two outdoor bathtubs to choose from."

My brows lift. "Wow. Maybe I've picked the wrong job. I mean, I love tattooing, but full-time taker of baths sounds like an amazing gig."

"I'm usually a shower guy, but right now, I'd be on board." He laugh-groans as we climb the steps onto the porch. "I could call my account Cranky Old Man in a Tub."

I hum beneath my breath. "Yeah, no. We can think of a better name for your account than that. I'll work on it while you're relaxing. Point me toward the fireplace, I'm a whiz with a fire. It's always my job at family functions. I get the firepits roaring while Melissa sets up the fire snacks station."

"Speaking of, I have s'mores supplies in the kitchen," he says, pausing to punch a code into the keypad on the back door. I didn't expect something so technological on an "off the grid" cabin, but it appears to be powered by a small solar cell on top of the device.

"Heck, yes," I say, my mouth watering at the thought. "Oh my God, toasted marshmallows sound so good right now. The only thing better would be a glass of wine."

As I follow him past a small, but simple dining table by the back door, into the partially renovated kitchen, it's like my words magically summon my wish into existence.

"What the..." Seven stops by the island at the end of the kitchen, staring at the large wicker basket on the coffee table in the small living room. It's filled with all sorts of treats, including a loaf of freshly baked bread from my favorite bakery in town, salami, popcorn, apples, oranges, bananas, and two bottles of wine—one white and one red.

"Looks like our kidnappers were worried about us going hungry," I say, still holding up my pants as I circle around Seven to pluck a card with our names on it from between two especially juicy-looking apples. I glance up at him with the envelope between two fingers. "Mind if I open this?"

He shakes his head. "No. But fair warning, this is making me even madder."

I arch a brow as I take in his stormy expression. "Noted. Maybe if you put down the bags, you'll feel less like punching something."

"Good point." He unburdens himself with stiff jerks of his arms before sagging to the ground and stretching out on the worn hardwood beside the coffee table. "My back needs a moment on a hard, flat surface. Traction would probably also be good."

I shake my head as I open the note. "You're definitely getting that bath. And a glass of wine while you're in there. You deserve it. Thank you, again, for carrying my pack."

"Never thank me for shit like that," he says, his eyes sliding closed. "You would have done the same thing."

I'm not certain I would have been *capable* of doing the same thing, but he's right—I would have tried. I may be a pint-sized hero compared to him, but I've always tried to be someone other people can count on in times of trouble.

I'm sure that's part of the reason Bettie did this. She was so grateful for what I did to help raise money for Sprout's surgery, and she knows I have a crush on her son. I've tried to hide it, but I'm not great with concealing my feelings, and Bettie reads people with the accuracy of a woman who's been a bartender-therapist for thirty years. She probably felt she had no choice but to help play matchmaker.

But when I open the card, the note inside isn't from Bettie.

It's from the other two members of this conspiracy...

"What's it say?" Seven asks, still stretched out on the floor with his eyes closed. Which is probably good. He should definitely be sitting down for this.

"Dear Binx and Seven," I read aloud, "Sorry we lied

and went to extremes, but you didn't give us a choice. Anyone with eyes can see that you're..." I clear my throat, a little embarrassed to read the next part, but muscling through. "Can see that you're perfect for each other. Hopefully three romantic days sharing a cabin in the woods will bring you to your senses. We've left all the supplies you'll need. There are snacks here in the basket, more food in the refrigerator, and clothes and toiletries in the drawers in the bedroom."

"I hate them," Seven rumbles from the floor, "but I'm not sad about a clean pair of clothes."

"Me either," I say, with a pointed look at my borrowed pants, which are currently rolled up on one side and tucked into my underwear to keep them from sliding down. Turning back to the card, I read on, "We put fresh sheets on the bed and left a speaker on the mantel with an old iPad loaded with songs, so you can play music. There's a charger in the basket, too. You should have everything you need, so please don't be stubborn goofballs and try to walk all the way back to Bad Dog or anything stupid like that."

Seven grunts.

"They know us, that's for sure," I reply before reading on, "Wendy Ann will be here to pick you up Friday morning. If you haven't realized you belong together by then, we promise we'll leave you alone to ruin your lives in peace. Love, Wendy Ann and Sprout (But mostly Sprout because this is my life you're trying to ruin, too. I love you guys, and I know you love each other. Please just kiss and live happily ever after already.)"

By the time I'm finished, my throat is tight, and I'm even sadder than I was before.

I wonder what Sprout would think if she knew we'd already kissed and all it had done was make Seven even more determined to push me away?

"Well, that's going to be a fun conversation," Seven mutters, his eyes closed again.

I don't ask him what he's talking about. I already know.

He's planning what to say to Sprout once he's home on Friday, how to tell her that her plan failed and there isn't going to be a happily ever after.

"At least we have food and shelter and don't have to walk the rest of the way home," I say, trying to look on the bright side. "I'm not sure my thighs could take two more days of hiking right now."

"And I can get some work done around here," he says. "It won't be a complete waste of time. I have everything I need to stain the new cabinets and get them hung above the sink."

His tone implies that it *will* be a partial waste of time, however, and about as much fun as getting his colon flushed.

I pride myself on my thick skin, but his tone gets to me for some reason. Maybe it's the exhaustion of the day or the pain from my wounds or just the fact that I'm madly in love with a man who acts like I'm a plague he's determined not to catch, but before I know it tears are stinging into my eyes.

I tuck the card back into the basket and circle quickly around Seven's prone form, hurrying toward the door before he gets a look at my face. "I'll go grab some kindling before it gets too dark and start the fire for bath water. Be back in a few."

I burst through the door without waiting for a response.

I head off the porch and into the woods a few dozen feet away, taking deep breaths and fighting to get control of myself. I shouldn't take any of this personally. Seven is a stubborn, independent man whose free will has been taken away. That's why he's cranky, not because he's repulsed by the thought of spending a few days alone with me.

He proved he wasn't repulsed by me with that kiss this morning and again when he was treating my wounds. I know I wasn't the only one affected by his hands on my thighs. Even when my skin was stinging with agony, the longing to get closer to him was still there.

In different circumstances, the tender way he caressed my leg before the bandages were in place would have been enough to make my panties wet.

Speaking of panties...

I can't wait to get a fresh pair on. Say what you will about our meddling family members, but at least they had the forethought to leave us extra clothes, just in case. I don't care if I have to take an ice-cold shower, I fully intend to be clean by the time Seven emerges from his bath.

I finish gathering a pile of small sticks to use as kindling, hitch my borrowed pants up with one hand, then scoop the pile up under my other arm. When I turn back toward the cabin, both of my hands are occupied.

Still, I usually would have been able to drop the sticks and lift my arms in time to fend off the beast hurling itself at my midsection.

I blame the twenty-mile hike for my slow reflexes and Seven's oversized pants for the fact that I trip on loose fabric as I step backwards and end up flat on my back in the fall leaves, making me easy prey for the fur potato leaping onto my chest.

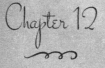

Chapter 12

SEVEN

I hear Binx squeal from the bedroom, where I'm scoping out the clothes Sprout packed for me, and spin toward the door. My aching muscles protest the swift movement, but I push through the pain and stiffness.

We may have food and clothing, but we don't have any cell service out here or any other way to call for help. If there's an emergency, things could go very bad, very quickly. It's something I'm going to be sure to impress upon Sprout as soon as we're home.

You can't just kidnap people and leave them stranded in the middle of nowhere without a way to reach medical attention. My mother and Binx's sister should have known better, and I intend to make sure my daughter doesn't grow up to make reckless decisions like this as a grown-up.

I push through the back door and charge out onto the deck.

It takes a beat for my eyes to adjust to the fading light outside, but after a moment, I spot Binx in the shadows beneath the trees and exhale a relieved breath.

"Don't worry, he's harmless," I say, dragging a hand through my hair as I slow my pace. "His name's Tater Tot. Just tell him to sit."

"He *is* sitting," Binx says, her voice strained. "On my chest, and his teeth are fucking enormous. He showed them to me a second ago."

"Aw, he was just smiling at you, no reason to be afraid," I say, chuckling when Tater Tot turns to grin at me, flashing his giant bottom teeth. "Isn't that right, you little charmer? I didn't know if I'd see you again before hibernation time. You're looking good, man. Nice and husky for the winter."

"Please, get him off of me?" Binx pleads as I stop a few feet away, gazing down at her with an amused grin. "I'm not a fan of rodents. Even really cute rodents that look like fur potatoes."

"Groundhogs are sweet, actually, especially this one," I say as I crouch down and cluck my tongue for Tater Tot. "I've known this guy since he was a baby last spring. I met him when we were first looking at the property. He's crazy smart. Understands his name, sit, and the names of all his favorite treats. Come here, Tater Tot. Come on, buddy. I'll grab you an apple slice from inside."

At the word "apple slice" Tater Tot scrambles off Binx's chest and trots over. He stops about a foot away from me, his entire pudgy bottom trembling with excitement. I don't hold a hand out to touch him, though.

Sprout desperately wanted to turn Tater Tot into another family pet, but the three chickens we have already are more than enough for me.

Tater Tot is better off in the wild, without the smell of human beings on him. It's best if he maintains a little fear of getting too close to us.

Though he *was* just sitting on Binx's chest...

I glance her way as she sits up, brushing furiously at the front of her fleece. "He's never climbed on top of anyone before. He usually keeps his distance."

"Really? He jumped at me like the killer bunny from that Monty Python movie." She stands, inching farther away from the trembling groundhog. "And when I tripped and fell, he was on me before I could move."

I frown. "Are you okay? Did you hurt yourself when you fell?"

She shakes her head. "No, just my pride. Logically, I know rodents can be sweet furry friends, but there's a reason I refuse to pet-sit Uncle Maynard's guinea pigs. I just can't with vermin. Even pet vermin." She shudders and shakes her hands at her sides. "I feel like I've been touched by the Black Death. It was spread by rats, you know."

"It was spread by fleas on rats," I correct as I back toward the cabin.

"Great, now I can worry about fleas," she mutters, brushing harder at her shirt.

"Don't stress," I say. "You can have the first bath and get out of your flea clothes. You have a whole drawer full of things in the bedroom. Why don't you go pick something out to wear, and I'll start the fire after I get Tater Tot his treat."

Tater Tot gambols along beside me, making happy grunting sounds.

"Okay," Binx says. "If you don't mind."

"Not at all. You can even circle around and head in the front door, if you want. The better to avoid another interaction with the feral fur potato."

Her lips quirk. "Sounds good."

Twenty minutes later, I've given Tater Tot his treat and sent him on his way back into the darkening forest. I also have five large pots of water about to bubble on the woodstove in the living room. I accompany Binx outside to fill the tub about a third of the way with cold water from the hose, and light the tiki torches I fished out of storage in the shed.

Then, we pull deck chairs to the edge of the flickering torchlight. I dump the first pots of boiling water into the tub and put another round on the stove before settling into the chair beside her to watch the stars come out.

"I feel bad about stealing your bath," she says as I hand her a glass of wine.

"You didn't steal it. I'll just take second shift."

"But it will take forever to warm up more water," she says. "The tub is enormous. There's plenty of room for both of us. We could wear our swimsuits and just...wash around them discreetly. It would be a totally kosher, time-and-effort saving thing for two friends to do."

I chew the inside of my cheek for a beat. I know better, but I'm bone weary and not looking forward to repeating this boiling water dance a second time or bathing in cold, leftover water.

"I'd stay on my side," she adds, lifting her right hand into the air. "I promise. I won't let so much as a pinkie toe slip over into your half of the water."

"I'm not worried about your pinkie toe," I say, hating that things are so awkward between us. That kiss ruined everything. I'd like to say that, if given the chance, I would turn back time and keep my lips to myself. But the truth is I'll be playing that kiss on repeat in my head for a long time.

A long, *long* time...

"Well, I'm worried about yours," she says, taking a delicate sip of her wine. "Your feet are disgusting."

I huff out a soft laugh. "Thanks."

"You're welcome. I mean, I know you can't help it—giant, manly men have giant, hairy man feet—but if you were a woman, you'd never get away with having something that gross on your body. Society would have made you wax them and bleach them and get big toe reduction surgery or something."

I smile. "You're probably right. Did I tell you Sprout asked me about shaving her legs last week?"

"What?" Binx frowns. "She's only eight."

"I know, but she inherited my hairy legs and the girls in gym class were making fun of her for it, calling her Sasquatch and shit. I told her she's too young to shave, but I caught her trying to smuggle my razor into her bathroom the next day. If I don't teach her how to use it, I'm afraid she's going to massacre herself." I sigh. "I really don't like being cut off from her. What if something happens and she needs to get in touch?"

Binx hums sympathetically. "Yeah, I get it. I don't like it, either, but she'll be fine. She has Bettie and your brothers to look after her if anything happens. And I can show her how to shave when we get back, if you want. There's definitely a trick to getting around all the bony parts without leaving a trail of destruction behind."

"Yeah, that would be nice, thanks," I say, even as the voice of reason insists that I should start distancing myself from Binx. She's too tempting for this "just friends" farce we've been playing at to hold much longer.

And I'm too lonely.

I didn't realize how lonely I was until she came into our lives and sending her home at the end of the night started to feel like the worst part of my day. It reminded me of the moment when visiting hours were over at the prison on Sundays, and the people I loved went away for another week, leaving me alone with the consequences of my piss poor decisions.

But I'm too tired to start the pulling away process right now, and I'm sure Sprout would much rather learn to shave from Binx than her grandmother. Mom is a stress case when it comes to her granddaughter's well-being and will appreciate being spared the task of crouching by a bathtub while Sprout tests out a razor for the first time.

"Should I go change into my suit, then?" Binx asks, arching a brow.

"Yeah, sure," I say. "I think we're almost good with

hot water. We don't want it too hot, or it will hurt your wounds."

She sighs. "Yeah, I thought about that. A shame, though, because a scalding hot bath sounds amazing. I can feel my muscle knots giving birth to new baby knots as we sit here, and I didn't carry two giant packs all day. If you want, I could get out first and then warm up more water for you to have a longer, hotter soak, after I'm done washing up."

"Don't worry about it. A warm bath is fine," I say. "Then, I'll probably turn in early. I found the old sheets that were on the bed before in the hamper in the closet. I'll use those to make up a bed on the couch and you can have the bedroom."

Her smile falters for half a second, but it's back in place again as she stands. "Okay, but I'm fine with taking the couch if you'd rather have the mattress. I can sleep anywhere, especially when I'm this exhausted."

She disappears inside without waiting for an answer.

I finish my glass of wine and check on the water, finding all but the largest pot beginning to bubble. I dump the four boiling containers and by the time I'm done, the biggest is ready to go, too. All in all, it takes about ten minutes to get it all sorted. By the time I'm done, the tub is over half full and steaming in the cool evening, but Binx still isn't back from changing.

I debate going to check on her, but she's good about calling for help when she needs it—or squealing if she's being attacked by overly-friendly groundhogs—so I grab my suit from my pack in the living room. I wouldn't normally have a suit with me for a hiking trip in the fall, but there was supposed to be a hot spring near our camping spot on the last night of the climbing trip.

If any of that itinerary was real...

Wondering how far my daughter went to trick me into this, and if the owner of the rock-climbing company has any idea her business was used as bait for a Parent Trap scheme, I pop into the bathroom and change. By the time I step out, wrapped in one of the large beach towels from this summer, when Sprout would entertain herself running through the sprinklers while I worked, I head outside.

I arrive on the deck in time to see Binx drop her own towel onto the deck chair she's pulled up beside the tub, revealing lacy black panties that stop me dead in my tracks. The lingerie rides high on her ass, covering only half of each cheek, the partial glimpse of skin somehow even sexier than if she were wearing a thong.

My gaze tracks down her toned, curvy legs and back up again. Then, she turns as she steps into the water, and I forget how to breathe.

Or maybe I gasp, I'm not sure.

I do something that attracts her attention because she looks up. Our eyes lock and hold in a moment of eye contact that would qualify as cheating if either of us were in a relationship.

But we're not, and fuck, she's the sexiest thing I've ever seen in that lacy bra and panties. I'm pretty sure I can see the dusky outline of her nipples through the lace, but I refuse to look.

I won't look.

I won't...

But I do, of course, I do. My weakness around this woman has already been proven several times today.

When I look back up to her face, her lips are curved in a crooked smile. "Sorry, looks like I forgot my swimsuit."

I try to swallow, but fail, and end up licking my lips instead. "It happens," I say, my voice rough.

"It does," she says, nodding her head. "Come get in. The water's perfect."

I start to drop my towel, but think better of it, in case the semi-hard-on I'm currently sporting becomes something more serious when I get closer to the siren easing into my bathtub. Instead, I keep it wrapped around my waist until I'm next to the water, then quickly chuck it and ease inside, keeping my gaze locked on the soap sitting in the dish attached to the side.

It's pale blue and smells incredible. It definitely isn't anything I purchased for the house. Before I can ask where it came from, Binx offers, "The soap was at the bottom of the basket. Guess our meddling family thought we might want to smell good for each other."

"You always smell good," I say, the words out before I can stop them.

"Liar," she whispers. "I smelled like a wet dog most of today."

"You smelled fine," I say. "You smelled...like you."

"And you smelled like you," she says, shifting onto her knees, bringing her now wet breasts bobbing above the surface. The lace is now completely see-through, and I'm fully erect beneath the water.

I can't stay here, or my hands will be on her, and I can't make a run for the door without her knowing exactly why I'm bolting. Still, I'm about to do it—let her see what a weak-willed bastard I am—when she shifts forward, her hands braced on either side of the tub beside me, bringing her lips inches from mine.

"And the smell of you is enough to make me wet," she whispers, making my jaw clench and my entire body burn. I want to touch her so badly it's physically painful, but I'm still determined to get out of this tub, when she adds, "That's why being friends isn't going to work anymore. I realized that as I was changing clothes and just seeing your boxer briefs sitting in a drawer made me want to touch myself."

"Binx," I rasp, her name a prayer for her to have mercy on me.

"I know you are firmly against being more than friends," she continues, "and I respect that. I don't agree with you, but...it's obvious you're not going to change your mind. So, it seems like our only choice is to go our separate ways."

I don't want to go our separate ways. I want to drag her to my bedroom and keep her there for the next thirty years, but I can't. It wouldn't be fair to either of us.

So, even though the words feel like they're ripping my heart out of my chest, I say, "You're probably right."

Sadness flashes across her pretty face, but it's gone by the time she nods and says, "I thought you'd agree. Which means there's only one thing left to decide." She shifts even closer, until her breasts are inches from my chest, her knees are between my thighs, and I'm so hard it feels like my balls might explode. "Do we spend the next two days avoiding each other as best we can while sharing a tiny cabin?" She leans in, brushing her nose against mine, her breath warm on my lips. "Or do we say goodbye with orgasms? I don't know about you, but I vote—"

Before she can finish the sentence, my fingers are around her neck, dragging her mouth against mine for a brutal kiss.

Chapter 13

BINX

I've always wanted a man to kiss me like he was starved for me, like he was near death and his only hope of survival lay in the friction of our mouths waging gentle war as we press closer, closer, straining to crawl inside each other's skin.

Seven is *definitely* kissing me like that.

Like he can't get enough of me, like he'll *never* get enough.

His tongue hot against mine, his beard prickling my chin, the way his fingers thread into my hair, cradling my head as he devours me—it's all electric. Intoxicating. Better than anything I could have imagined before the moment his lips met mine.

I arch closer, pressing my breasts against his chest, moaning as the friction from the wet lace sends another jolt of arousal straight between my legs. I don't feel my wounds at all anymore. When I first stepped into the water, there was a little stinging, but now I'm too high on endorphins to care.

I've never been this turned on this fast.

A part of me is ready to strip out of my panties and straddle him beneath the water, but the other part knows better than to rush. If this is the only time I get to be with Seven, I want to make it last.

I want to remember every magical second...

Pulling back the slightest bit, easing off the gas, I run my hands over the crisp hairs on his chest, relishing the powerful feel of him beneath my palms. His lips leave mine, searing a trail across my jawline as his fingers mold to my ribs just beneath the surface of the water.

"You taste like the forest," he rumbles into my ear, making me shiver and my nipples tighten until they're burning for his touch.

"I guess that's a good thing?" I murmur, biting my lip to hold back another moan as he drops one hand to squeeze my ass beneath the water.

"It's a perfect thing, real and wild," he says, dragging his teeth lightly along my throat before he adds, "I'm pretty sure I want to fuck you more than I've ever wanted anything in my life."

I exhale a turned-on sound of relief that becomes a groan as he pulls my panties to one side and pushes two fingers deep inside me. "Oh God, Seven," I gasp, shivers of pleasure vibrating from my core to the tips of my fingers and toes. "Yes, I want you so much."

"So wet," he murmurs as he kisses me again, the glide of his tongue against mine slower now, matching the sensuous rhythm of his hand as he fucks me slow and deep. "I can feel you all over my fingers, even under the water. Do you want me that much, baby?"

"Yes," I say, my voice trembling. "I want you more than anything. And I want you bare, nothing but you."

He groans. "You're so damned sexy. I want to fill every inch of you." He emphasizes the words by driving his fingers even deeper, making my head spin.

I want that, too, so fucking much, and he will *absolutely* fill every inch. I've only brushed up against his erection a few times under the water, but it's enough to confirm he's as big there as he is everywhere else. But I'm not the least bit concerned. He's right, I'm already drenched for him and it's only getting worse with every touch, every kiss.

I'm ready for him.

Ready for him to bury himself deep and ruin me for other men.

I already know no other man will ever compare to him, to the way he sets my body and soul ablaze as he whispers against my lips, "I've been tested. I'm clear for STDs, and I've had the vasectomy, so we don't have to worry about pregnancy, so..." He leaves his fingers buried deep this time, pulsing against my inner walls as he rubs his thumb in gentle circles around my clit. "Is it okay if I come inside you? I really want to fill this hot little pussy up with my come."

Digging my fingers into his shoulders, I fight to pull in a breath as the tension building low in my body pulses higher, tighter. "Yes," I gasp, panting and trembling as he does an undulating thing with his fingers that makes my brain come unglued. "Oh yes. Yes, God, Seven, I want that. Now. Please, oh God."

I come crying out his name and something about

how boneless he makes me feel that is probably weird, but he doesn't care. He knows I'm weird. It's one of the things he likes about me.

Loves about me...

He loves me, I know he does, it's there in the glow in his eyes as he coaxes me down from my release, whispering, "You're so fucking beautiful, Binx. Fuck, woman, you destroy me. Watching you get into the tub..." He exhales a ragged breath. "I almost came for you right then. I wanted to rip these panties down your thighs, bend you over the tub, and devour you. I can't wait to eat your pussy. I want your salt all over my face. I want your taste imprinted on my fucking tongue."

I emit a soft whimper that isn't like me. I'm usually pretty bold in bed, but I've never had a man talk to me like this before.

"What the hell, Mr. Dirty Talk?" I ask as he pulls his fingers from inside me. "Where did you come from?"

His lips curve into a wicked smile as his hands skim up my waist to the bra clasp between my shoulders. "Hell, McGuire, you haven't seen anything yet."

Then, he proceeds to prove it.

In seconds, my bra has vanished and his mouth is doing things to my breasts that make me throw my head back and beg the moon for mercy. Clinging to him in the warm water as he licks and sucks and bites my nipples, with the stars spinning overhead and a cool fall breeze electrifying my already sensitized skin, I know sex doesn't get better than this. It's just like Seven said—it's real and perfect.

As natural as breathing...

When he lifts me out of the water, guiding me onto my knees with my forearms braced on one end of the tub, I don't hesitate for a moment. This feels like a dance we've done a hundred times before. And yes, a part of me would have liked to be face-to-face for our first time, but it's safer this way. I'm so wet and ready for him, but with enough friction under the water, we could run into trouble with lubrication. And that's a no go.

Once we get started, I already know I'm not going to want to stop.

Not ever.

"Yes, yes," I cry out in encouragement as he fits himself to my entrance from behind and slowly pushes inside. The head of his cock is so thick, it stretches me to my limit, but I love it, love *him*. "More," I beg.

"You're so tight," he says, his voice strained. "I don't want to hurt you."

"You aren't. You won't," I promise, wiggling my hips a little, thrilling to feel another half inch of him slip inside. "You feel amazing, and I told you, I'm not made of glass."

"I know you're not," he says as he braces a hand beside mine on the edge of the tub and brings his lips to my shoulder. "You're made of magic."

The words might have been cheesy from someone else, but the way Seven says them—so matter-of-fact, so sincere—makes them the best thing I've ever heard. His groan of pleasure-pain-relief-joy as he pushes all the way inside me a second later is a close second.

"Oh, God, baby," he says, the endearment hitting me

straight in my soul as he begins to move. "You're so perfect, so fucking perfect."

I've had men call me "baby" before, and I've pretty quickly encouraged them to find another pet name—or just go with Binx for fuck's sake. I don't find being infantilized sexy, but it isn't like that when Seven calls me "baby." It's not about making me something smaller, or less-than, it's about expressing how precious I am to him.

This man would die to protect me, give up anything to keep me safe, I feel it in every stroke of his body into mine. He's rough and hungry, but also careful, every ounce of his focus on me, making sure I can take everything he has to give.

And I can...

It's what I was made for, to be with him like this, to be his baby and for him to be mine.

"Don't hold back," I beg, covering his hand and holding on tight as I push back against his next thrust. I turn over my shoulder, kissing him hard as he holds still inside me. I kiss him with all the wild, feral love I feel for him, before panting against his lips, "Give me all of you. I want it all. Trust me, I can handle it, Seven. I promise I can."

His forehead pressed to mine and his arm locked tight around my waist, he gives me his trust. He pulls back and slams into me again, fucking me with the training wheels off, no guardrails, no limits. He takes me like an animal, both of us groaning and gasping and doing our best to fuck our way into each other's skin, until my orgasm explodes inside me like a bomb.

Pleasure forks hot through my molten core. I'm on fire with it, and I've never been so happy to burn.

I'm still throbbing in a dizzy pink haze, aftershocks rippling through me, when he shoves deep and comes inside me with a savage sound that makes me wish we could do it all over again this very second. I arch my spine, sealing us even closer as his cock pulses against my walls and the heat of his release fills me up.

I don't know if it's the fact that it's the first time a man has ever come inside me without protection—or if it's just Seven—but the feel of it is enough to send me spinning out all over again.

This orgasm isn't as violent, but it's deep, profound, rattling my bones and rearranging the stars. By the time I finally come back to myself, I'm lying on Seven's chest in the water. My back is to his front and he's gently running the soap over my bare body, careful not to touch my pleasure-raw parts just yet.

I shift my head until I can look up and see his profile silhouetted against the night sky. I sigh, but don't say a word, not feeling like I need to. It feels like everything that needed to be said was expressed when he clung to me like a lifeline as he came.

Seven turns, kissing my forehead before setting the soap aside and scooping the cooling water over me with his big hand. "How many times do you think we can do that before Friday morning?" he finally asks.

I clench my jaw and take a breath, willing away the flash of pain in my chest. A part of me hoped the fantastic sex would have changed his mind, but I'm not surprised that it didn't. He's stubborn, especially when he thinks he's doing the right thing.

But walking away from a connection like this isn't right, it's madness.

Hopefully, a few days of explosive orgasms will be enough to prove that to him.

"Four hundred," I say in a husky, pleasure-drunk voice that makes him smile.

"Might be a little ambitious, but I'm game," he says, meeting my gaze as I shift over to sit on the other side of the tub. His brow furrows slightly, but before he can say whatever vibe-killing thing I'm sure is on the tip of his tongue, I splash him with the soapy water.

"Me, too," I say, "but not in cold water. You'd better hurry up and get clean before your toes freeze off. I'll dry off and meet you inside." I stand, letting the water roll down my body for a beat. The way his eyes devour me is worth the chill as the fall breeze kisses my skin. "I'll be the one naked by the fire."

His jaw clenches. "I'll be the one ready to fuck you again."

I grin. "Good. That's how I like you."

I step out of the tub, wrapping up in my towel and padding barefoot back into the cabin, not even the sight of Tater Tot lurking in the shadows like a creepy little fur potato voyeur is enough to cool my excitement for the night ahead.

So, a groundhog watched our first time? So what?

Next time, we're going to be all alone, nothing but Seven and me and the fire warm on our skin and two whole days of magic stretching out in front of us.

It'll be enough to change his mind.

I believe that—I have to believe it, because the thought of living the rest of my life without that man's body wrapped around mine isn't okay.

Not even close.

Chapter 14

SEVEN

My first thought when I wake up with Binx spooned against me is that this is probably the dumbest decision I've ever made.

I'm going to regret every second of these few stolen days with her as soon as we get home.

By this time next week, I'll be kicking myself, wishing I had no idea how good it feels to wake up with her in my bed, to be buried inside her sweetness.

But right now?

Fuck... I'm happy.

The happiest I've been in longer than I can remember.

"Again?" she murmurs, laughter in her voice as I wake her with my hand down the front of her panties and my erection nudging the small of her back.

We were at it until one in the morning last night, transitioning from her riding me in front of the fireplace to writhing together between the sheets, but the lack of sleep has done nothing to take the edge off my need for her.

"I mean, we could wait until after breakfast," I say, kissing her neck, marveling at the softness of her skin. She feels like rose petals under my lips, so soft and sexy. "If you're too tired and need fuel."

"I'm never too tired for you inside me," she says, reaching back to rub my cock through my boxer briefs, making me groan. "I was dreaming about you all night."

"Yeah? Anything you'd like for me to make a reality?" I ask as she rolls over, pressing a kiss to my bare chest that sends warmth surging through my entire body.

She's so damned sweet, and so perfectly filthy, a fact she proves by whispering, "I've never had anyone finger my ass while they were inside me before. But I've heard it's pretty great."

"That's a dream I can absolutely make come true," I promise her, before stripping off her pajamas. Flannel goes flying into the air and then her panties are down her thighs and I'm back where I belong.

It's a dangerous thought—this is only a stolen moment, nothing more—but I can't deny how right it feels to guide her legs over my shoulders and cradle her ass in my hands as I devour her pussy. She tastes like hope and secrets and white water roaring through a mountain pass and when she comes on my face, I groan and relish the rush of her on my lips like a baptism.

Seconds later, I'm inside her, grinding into her pulsing heat as I tell her how beautiful she is, how fucking sexy. She clings to me, trembling with after-shocks from her first orgasm as I glide my hand through the slickness on her thighs, guiding it back to ease the passage of my finger as I tease into the tight ring of her ass.

"Oh, wow. Yeah, that feels amazing," she murmurs, shivering as she wraps her arms tighter around my neck. Her teeth rake across my throat as she bite-kisses me, murmuring, "More. I can take more."

"Greedy woman," I say, but I love it. I love how hungry she is for me, how she craves wild, primal fucking as much as I do.

How she abandons herself to me, giving me her trust without holding back.

I never want to betray that trust. I tell myself that I won't, that she's the one who suggested this particular breed of farewell, and she's a woman who knows her own mind. But as she comes, her body pulsing around my finger and my cock with a ferocity that leaves me no choice but to bury myself deep and empty my balls in this gorgeous woman, I'm not sure.

"I never want to hurt you," I whisper against her cheek as we catch our breath.

She reaches up, pressing her finger to my lips. "Don't be silly. Your finger isn't that big. That was incredible by the way."

I pull back, gazing down into her face. She looks... determined. There's little doubt in my mind that she's deliberately misunderstanding me, but still, I feel obligated to say, "You know that's not what I meant."

"I know," she says briskly. "But I'm fine, I promise. I'm fine now, and I'll be fine in the future." She exhales a soft laugh, a smile curving her lips as she adds, "I mean, I think I will. Assuming you feed me soon. I'm starving. I'm not used to this much cardio before breakfast."

I grin, ignoring the regret trying to take root inside me. I refuse to regret this or spend a second of our time together worrying about what happens after. We made this decision together, with our eyes wide open. Thinking about the future is only going to ruin the here and now.

Which would be a damned shame, because the here and now is fucking incredible.

Binx joins me in the bathroom, washing up in the freezing cold shower, giggling and teasing me about the amount of shrinkage going on below my nonexistent belt. I tease her about her diamond-hard nipples before taking one into my mouth to "warm it up."

Before I know it, we're fucking against the bathroom wall, Binx clinging to my shoulders as I take her hard and deep. We come seconds apart and I sag against the plaster, letting it hold us up as I will strength back into my knees.

Binx laughs again and squeezes my butt. "We should do that again in here. The view of your ass in the mirror while you're pumping inside me is...chef's kiss."

I pull back, gazing into her flushed face. "Yeah?"

She nods. "Oh yeah. You really put your back into it."

I grin. "Thanks. I try."

"You succeed," she assures me, pressing a kiss to my cheek that I feel in every one of my sex-shaken cells. "Now, we really have to eat. No more fun and games. I think my stomach is eating itself."

I pull an exaggerated frown. "A cannibalistic stomach. That sounds serious."

She nods. "Very. Our only hope is to fill it with blueberries from the fridge ASAP." She squeezes my ass again before adding in a playful voice, "And then to give it all the pancakes and bacon it can eat. But I can't make them because I'm already too weak to cook."

I laugh. "You're always too weak to cook."

She sighs. "I know. It's a flaw, one of my very few flaws, I might add. But, as you know, I'm very appreciative of all food that's cooked for me, and heap on the praise as I eat. So, I think it all balances it out."

It more than balances out, and I love cooking for her. I love it at home, when I'm busy in the kitchen and she and Sprout are finishing up homework at the table, and I love it even more this morning, with Binx dancing around the kitchen to Van Morrison playing on the speaker as I flip pancakes. I can't remember the last time I smiled this much, laughed this much, felt this free to relish how good it feels to be alive.

When she presses against me, distracting me with a kiss as she steals a piece of freshly fried bacon from the plate beside me, my chest bubbles over with something more than happiness.

Joy...that's what this is.

It's been a while since it filled me up like this, like a spring pumping from deep in the earth with no sign of stopping.

It's going to be a good day, there's no doubt about that.

Maybe one of my best days ever...

Chapter 15

BINX

I've been in love with Seven for a while, but now I'm pretty sure I'm addicted to his body, his touch, his kiss.

To the way he looks at me across the picnic table as we linger over the world's longest breakfast beneath the autumn leaves...

Saying goodbye is going to be hell, but I refuse to think about that now, not while he's grinning at me in the sunshine as he sneaks bacon from my plate.

"That's mine, mister," I say, narrowing my eyes in mock anger. "You should ask before you steal a girl's bacon."

"Then it wouldn't be stealing," he says, his eyes dancing as he pops my last bite into his mouth. "I promise, I'll make it up to you."

I arch a teasing brow, loving that I don't have to fight the urge to flirt with him anymore. "Oh yeah? How are you going to do that? Especially if you're working on staining cabinets all day?"

He hums low in his throat. "Maybe I could be convinced to leave the cabinets for another day and take you on an adventure instead."

I sit up straighter, every cell in my body perking up. "Now, you're talking. What kind of adventure?" I wrinkle my nose as I add, "As long as it doesn't involve too much walking. My wowies are much better, but a long walk probably isn't a great idea."

He smiles, a fond grin that makes me want to crawl across the table and into his arms. "Wowies... You've been spending too much time with Sprout."

"I like that she calls them wowies. Much more badass than owie. Makes a wound sound like a badge of honor."

"It does," he agrees. "I was thinking we could take the four-wheeler out to a place I know. I checked this morning and our kidnappers forgot to empty the gas tank. We still have enough left to get us halfway to Bad Dog if we wanted."

I bite my lip. "But you don't want...do you? I know I don't."

He shakes his head as he reaches across the table, looping his fingers around my wrist. "No, I don't. I want to soak up every second I have left with you."

The reminder that we have an expiration date brings us both down for a second, but then Seven adds, "And I want to fuck you in one of my favorite places in the world," and my blood starts buzzing again.

I lean in, asking, "In the outdoors? Isn't that kind of scandalous?"

"The bathtub is outdoors."

"Well, yes, but it's on a porch, close to a house. That's

almost indoors. And it was dark out. Getting busy in the middle of the day in the woods is another thing entirely. There could be game cameras anywhere. You never know."

He winks. "Who said it was in the woods?"

I arch a brow. "Um, look around. There's nothing but woods around here. It has to be in the woods."

"Does it?" He turns my hand over, tracing a line up my wrist to my forearm with his finger that makes me burn. "Guess you'll just have to wait and see. You'll want to pack a sweatshirt. I know it's weirdly warm today, but it might not be where we're going."

I tap my foot beneath the table, my thoughts racing. "Might not be where we're going... Is it a cave? It's a cave, isn't it?"

He shakes his head. "I'm not telling."

"It has to be a cave. That's the only logical explanation for why it would be colder and not in the forest. But it has to be a cave without bats, okay? Tessa and Wesley had to get rabies shots after they went crawling around in a cave with bats. It sounded horrific. It was like...half a dozen shots spread out over a month or something."

His smile widens. "Head back and grab your sweatshirt and the water bottles. I'll check on the four-wheeler and meet you in the shed."

I scrunch my face into an expression of exaggerated irritation. "No bats. I'm serious. I can't deal with bats. Rabies is serious business, and they're way too rodent adjacent. They're basically rats with wings, and I've already been attacked by a groundhog."

"Attacked might be a strong word," he says, releasing

my hand and rising from his side of the table. "Tater Tot was just trying to be friendly." He leans in, lowering his voice as he begins to stack our plates. "Don't look now, but I think he's still a fan of yours. He's been hiding out in the leaves over there eyeing your tasty backside for a while now."

I flinch and spin to look behind me, making Seven laugh.

Once I'm sure the leaves are groundhog-free, I spin back to him, smacking his arm as I stand. "What a jerk you are. Making fun of my rodent phobia isn't funny."

"Kind of funny," he says. "I've never seen you afraid of anything before. It's a novel experience."

"I'm afraid of lots of things," I say, stacking our coffee mugs on top of the plates. "I'm just good at hiding it most of the time."

He sobers, his brow furrowing. "Like what? And why do you hide it?"

I shrug, but hold his gaze as I ask, "I don't know, why do any of us hide our weak spots? The world isn't really a safe place for weakness. I mean, you hide your weak spots, too."

"What weak spots?" he quips with that easy grin I'm coming to love.

He should grin like that more often, but only for me.

When I shoot him a narrow look, he tips his head in acknowledgement of the fact that he might have a weak spot or two. "Yeah, I do. But it's not socially acceptable for men to be weak. Not in the circles I run in anyway."

"It isn't okay for women to be weak, either. Not anymore," I say. "But it's also not okay to be too strong.

When you are, you become a target for people who don't like girls who color outside the lines. They want to crush your will to live before it gets too strong for their liking. That can be shitty, even scary, sometimes." I shrug. "But I'm not going to stop being myself because a chunk of the world would like me better if I shut my mouth and played by their stupid rules."

"Fuck 'em, you're perfect, just the way you are." He leans over, pressing a kiss to my cheek before whispering, "And in my book? Strong is sexy as hell."

"Good to know," I whisper back, wishing he would forget about the four-wheeler and take me on the picnic table.

"See you in a few. And I promise, no bats." He grins as he pulls away and starts toward the shed. I force a smile, too, but it only lasts as long as it takes for him to turn his back on me.

Then I suck in a breath and fight the urge to fall apart.

Because that? Those things he just said?

It's everything I've wanted a man to say to me my entire life. It's what I've wanted my parents to say to me, too, but that's a whole other load of psychological baggage I'm too overwhelmed to think about right now.

God, why can't he see that he's everything I need? Everything I want and could ever wish for?

I don't care about the age gap. I don't care that he doesn't want more children or that I'd be getting a kid as well as a husband if we ended up going all the way together.

I love Sprout. I adore every piece of her crazy,

meddling, bossy, beautiful little self. Getting to help raise her would be an honor I wouldn't take lightly. I may be young, but I grew up in a big family with tons of cousins. I know what a huge responsibility it is to raise a child. I'd be going into the stepmom gig with my eyes wide open.

Surely, there has to be a way to get through to Seven.

Surely, all the red hot fuckery going on around here might wear him down at least a little. Because...woah, is it wearing on me. I thought I'd had some pretty fantastic sex in my life, but nothing I've done with anyone else can compare to the way I feel when Seven's hands are on me, when his gaze is locked on mine as he fills me.

And his cock? It's an enchanted love wand of unparalleled spectacular-ness so magical, that not even calling it something dorky like a "love wand" can diminish it's fantasticness in any way.

The thought of his love wand—*my* love wand—going on to fuck other women makes me want to burn down the world. I mean, I knew I had a jealous side, but this is crazy. As I went to sleep last night, a part of me was already planning ways to ensure Pammy is never alone with Seven again. I'll put a tracking device on her car and tail her around town if I have to.

I mean, I won't actually do that—I'm not insane— but I'm not above using underhanded methods to keep the thirsty women of Bad Dog at bay. Surely, Pammy, an older woman with no kids, would prefer a man without a young child she would have to help raise. I could sneakily set her up with one of my guy friends whose kids are already out of the house. None of them are half as hot as Seven, but Sprout isn't going to make things pleasant for anyone her dad might decide to date who isn't me. I know that kid, and she's as stubborn as her father and even more determined to get her way.

A nice, slightly-less-hot boyfriend without a daughter who puts Nair in your shampoo bottle and chicken poop in your purse might start looking pretty good to Pammy after a while...

"Get a grip," I mutter to myself as I drop the dirty dishes in the sink inside, grab a sweatshirt from the bureau, then head back into the kitchen to fill our water bottles. "You can't go full stalker on him. You promised you'd say goodbye after Friday. That was the deal, and you never go back on a deal."

I don't. I'm a woman of my word.

I guess I'll just have to hope all the fun we're having will change Seven's mind. And if not, at least we'll go out with a bang.

Several bangs, in fact...

I'm almost done filling the water bottles when Seven is suddenly behind me, his arms wrapped around my waist and his erection pressed into the hollow of my spine. "I'm sorry," he says, into my hair. "I'm a sick fuck who can't go ten minutes without being inside you. Just tell me to get off you, and I'll pull my shit together, I promise."

"Don't get off me," I say, arching my back until my ass rubs against his balls. "Get off *in* me. I was just thinking about how much I wanted you to take me on the picnic table when we were outside."

"Fuck, woman, you should have said something."

"Next time, I will," I say, gasping as he drags his teeth across the skin at my neck.

A beat later, his hands are up my shirt, dragging my bra down beneath my breasts. He plays with my nipples, making me gasp as I shove my leggings and underwear down to my knees. I reach back, fumbling for the close of his pants, then give up and tug them down as best I can, freeing his long, hot length with shaking hands.

I'm literally shaking. I want him *that* much.

We had sex less than an hour ago. I shouldn't be this hungry for him again already, but...I am. This man does things to me, things no man has ever done before, and I'm guessing none will ever do again. I can't imagine feeling this way about anyone else. This mixture of easy friendship and combustible chemistry isn't something you find every day.

It's rare. Precious.

Worth fighting for...

"Yes, oh God, yes," I cry out as he fits his cock to my entrance and shoves inside me, fast and hard.

And deep...so fucking deep.

I love how he fills every inch of me, until it's almost too much, until it almost hurts, but doesn't, because all he has to do is look at me and I'm soaked for him.

"Binx, fuck, baby," he moans against my neck as he braces one hand on the counter and wraps the other around my waist, holding me tight as he pistons inside me. "I can't get enough of you. You drive me fucking crazy."

"Me, too," I say, arching my back, taking him even deeper.

"Your body, your smell, your taste," he says, biting the place where my neck meets my shoulder, his teeth digging in deeper as he groans and fucks me harder.

It's animalistic and raw and gets me going like no quickie I've ever had before. The second he slides his hand from my waist to touch my clit, I explode, screaming out my orgasm into the quiet morning air, waves of pleasure stealing my breath away. He continues to grind the heel of his hand against my most electric, sensitive place, as he takes me with increasingly wild thrusts. Soon, I'm sagged against the counter, barely able to stand as I come again.

Seven joins me a second later, his cock jerking inside me as he groans sweet and filthy things about how much he loves coming inside my tight little pussy into my hair.

Afterwards, we remain folded over the counter for a long moment, catching our breath until I feel hot liquid slither down my thigh. "I should grab a paper towel," I say, reaching for the roll on the other side of the sink with a pleasure-limp arm.

"No, let me," he says, pressing a final kiss to my shoulder.

Then, he reaches for the paper towels, wets one with a bit of cool water from the sink, and cleans my thighs and the tops of my bandages with a gentle attention to detail that's every bit as charming as his feral, sex beast side. The fact that he has that inside him, and it coexists so peacefully with his nurturing self, is my personal romantic kryptonite.

If I weren't in love with him already, I would be by the time he tidies my sensitive sex with tender swipes of the cloth, finishing with a kiss to my ass cheek that makes me smile.

"Thanks for the help," I say, as he tosses the paper towel in the trash beneath the sink and stands to wrap his arms around me again from behind. "But I should probably pull up my pants."

"Never," he says, his hand coming to rest low on my bare stomach, just above where my belly becomes something more intimate. "You don't need pants. Your pussy told me she enjoys the open air, and being free and ready to fuck me at a moment's notice."

I snort. "Oh, she did, did she? What else did she say?"

He hums, and kisses my cheek, making my soul glow a little brighter before he says, "That my cock is her favorite cock."

"No lies detected," I murmur, "but there's one problem with this story."

"And what's that?"

"My pussy isn't a she. She's a he, and his name is Jerry."

"Jerry?" he asks.

"Yeah," I say, fighting a smile with everything in me. "Jerry. You have a problem with the name Jerry?"

"No, not at all," he says, playing along. "Just kind of a straight-laced name for a wild little pussy like her—I mean *him*, excuse me. But who am I to judge?"

"Exactly," I say, huffing in surprise when Seven gives the patch of hair on my mound a little smack. "What was that for?"

"It was a high five," he says. "For Jerry. So that he knows I still want to be special friends."

I bite my lip, nearly losing it. "Yeah? You don't mind that he's a boy?"

"Nah, I don't care. Love is love, right? And what Jerry and I have is too special to be destroyed by something as silly as whether he's a boy pussy or a girl pussy."

My smile fading a little, I say, "Well, good. Jerry's happy to hear that. So am I."

It's fun being silly with Seven, but hearing him toss the "L" word around in a joking way is hard to take. The "L" word isn't a joke for me. I "L" word Seven even more now than I did five minutes ago, and I have a feeling it's only going to get worse.

By the time Wendy Ann picks us up on Friday morning, I'll be like one of those lovesick Victorian women who locked themselves up in their crumbling mansions and wasted away from a broken heart.

No, you're not. We don't waste away; we rise and fight, a voice whispers in my head as Seven finally allows me to pull up my pants and we get our water bottles ready to go. *You still have time.*

The inner voice is right.

This isn't over until it's over, and I haven't even begun to fight.

Chapter 16

SEVEN

The only thing better than the best view in the world?

Having someone you love beside you to share it with.

I love this woman. I love her so much, I'm probably going to have to have a lobotomy to forget about how incredible it feels to be with her. But I'm a firm believer in the maxim that if you love something, you have to set it free.

Binx deserves to be free to find a man who's closer to her own age, who can give her everything she wants, including children and a life partner who can keep up with her for the next twenty to thirty years. The memories we're making right now are all we'll ever have, so I'm determined to enjoy the hell out of these two days with the sexiest, funniest, best woman in the world.

"So, what do you think?" I ask. "Does the surprise live up to the hype?"

Binx turns to look at me over her shoulder, her eyes

shining and the afternoon sun catching the red in her dark brown hair, making it glow around her face.

She's so fucking stunning, I lose the ability to process language as she replies, and have to ask her, "Sorry, I..." I shake my head, hoping to clear it. "Can you say that again?"

She swallows, her throat working before she says, "It's stunning, Seven. I had no idea there was a view like this anywhere around here." She glances back over the edge of the bluff overlooking the gorge below and the rock formations on the other side. "It's just...gorgeous. No pun intended."

With the river winding through the center of the valley below and the clear day making the view stretch on for at least a hundred miles, my lookout spot is really showing off. Still, when I showed Sprout this same view a few weeks ago, she wasn't impressed. She agreed it was pretty, then promptly asked if we could hike down to the bottom of the waterfall and look for salamanders in the pool below.

But she's just a kid. Kids take beautiful things for granted sometimes. They can't help it. They haven't had enough experience with the ugliness in life to realize how truly special beauty is.

"This is church to me," Binx whispers, a reverence in her tone that makes my chest ache. She gets it. She really does. "This is what you're supposed to feel in church, just...humbled by the beauty of creation and how lucky we are to get to live in it, even for a little while."

"Yeah." I loop my arm around her waist, my soul exhaling a sigh of relief when she leans into me, resting her head on my shoulder. "If church was like this, I wouldn't have snuck out the back every Sunday to smoke in the woods with my friends."

"Gross," she says with a soft laugh. "I can't believe you smoked as a kid."

"Says the woman who smokes as an adult," I say, pinching the side of her hip.

"I don't smoke, not really. I have a sweetly-scented clove cigarette once in a great while, as a source of comfort in times of trial. It's different."

"Why do they give you comfort?"

She hums, seeming to consider the question. "I don't know. Maybe because it reminds me of being a teenager out on the roof, daydreaming of a time when I'd be free to live my life however I wanted to live it." She chuckles. "Or maybe because smoking drives my parents absolutely batshit crazy, and a part of me really loves doing things to annoy them? Even if they don't know about it? Probably something mature like that."

I grunt. "I get that. I think I smoked for some of the same reasons. And because I was a twelve-year-old idiot."

"Ugh, you're right. I should outgrow it. Maybe I will someday, when the last of my stash is gone. You can't buy cloves in the U.S. anymore. I have to order them from overseas in bulk and store them in my freezer to keep them from going bad. It's a whole thing."

"Why can't you buy them in the U.S.?" I ask, sincerely worried now. "Because they're even worse than normal cigarettes?"

"Oh, yeah," she says without missing a beat, "they're

awful for you. Really super bad, tons of tar and all that garbage."

"Then stop, please. Right now. I need you to take good care of this gorgeous body," I say, adding when she laughs, "And what about Jerry? How is he going to get around if you're too busy wheezing to take him to see cool things?"

She looks up at me, a wry smile twisting her lips. "Okay, fine. I'll quit. I'll toss them when I get home. Are you happy now?"

I grin and drop my hand lower, squeezing the side of her fine ass. "Yes, I am. Thank you. What about you? Having a good day so far?"

"I'm having the best day," she says, with a sincerity that warms me all over. It's such a simple day, but it's one of the best I can remember, too. "But it would be even better if we could sneak down for a better look at that waterfall I can hear splashing away down there."

My head falls back as I laugh.

"What?" she says, smacking my chest. "I can do it! I have my good climbing shoes on and my thighs barely hurt at all under the bandages." She arches a sassy brow. "Also, I would like to point out that you weren't worried about my injuries when you were getting busy between my legs, Mr. Sex Beast."

"Yes, I was. I was being mindful of your wowies, I promise." I pull her fully against me, molding my hands to her ass as I pin her hips to mine. "I wasn't laughing about that. I was laughing because that's the same thing Sprout said when I brought her here. She spent about five seconds taking in the view, then wanted to hike down and look for salamanders."

Binx smiles. "Did you find any?"

"No. It was too late in the year, and it gets a lot colder down there in the gorge. I told her that, but she wouldn't listen." I sigh, the thought of my headstrong daughter taking a hint of the shine off the afternoon. "She's really good at that. Always has been, even before the accident."

Binx brushes a few loose hairs back into my ponytail. "Well, she comes by it honestly, Stubborn Human."

I fight the urge to lean into the hand she presses to my face and lose the battle. "She's going to be pissed."

I don't have to say what she'll be pissed about.

We both know.

"Let's go," Binx whispers after a beat. "It's been too long since I've felt waterfall spray on my face."

We hike down the right side of the gorge, sticking to the sunlit side of the path, and in just a few minutes, Binx's wish is granted.

"Smell that," she says, lifting her nose into the air as she closes her eyes. "It smells like the world is brand new again. God, I love fall. I know it's supposed to signal the end of things, but it always feels like a beginning to me."

I watch her basking in the sun, with rainbows forming around her from the waterfall mist, and for the first time in a long time, wish I had my phone. I'm old enough to remember what freedom felt like pre-internet age, and resent the shit out of my cell most of the time, but I would pay a pretty penny for an easily portable camera right now. I want to capture her just like this, beautiful and unguarded in her enjoyment of this simple moment.

Instead, I settle for imprinting it into my brain. I do my best to memorize every dip and curve of her face, from the elegant swoop of her full lips to the half-moons of her closed eyes.

When she opens them, I keep staring, getting lost in the flawless blue.

She smiles, a shy smile that isn't like her, but that I instantly love nearly as much as I love her big, bold grin. "You look really pretty right now."

My lips curve. "I was just thinking the same thing about you."

She laughs. "We should start a mutual admiration society. Or, better yet, a sketch club. I'm supposed to be teaching you to draw, remember? We haven't had a lesson in weeks."

The words remind me of the dozens of sketches of her lips in my sketch book. I'll have to hide that away when I get home. Looking at Binx's mouth is going to be painful for a while.

Probably a damn long while.

"We can do some sketching tonight," I say, starting back down the trail, putting the sad thought aside. "I don't have pencils or pastels, but I have plenty of ball-point pens and blank paper. You could teach me how to draw bowls and plates or something after dinner."

"And I'll make you pose nude for me while you practice," she says, making me snort as I toss a glance over my shoulder.

"Only if you do the same," I say, loving—and hating

—the idea of drawing her naked. That's a sketch that would come back to haunt me later, no doubt in my mind.

"I absolutely will," she says as we reach the bottom of the waterfall and step onto the cool stones in the shade beneath it. "I'm not afraid of a little nudity."

She proves it by stripping off her shirt and reaching for the top of her leggings.

I arch a brow. "You aren't getting in the water."

She grins. "Yes, I am. Life's too short not to skinny dip in every waterfall possible."

"You'll freeze your ass off," I warn her.

She shrugs as she steps out of her leggings and under-wear, kicking them off and leaving them on the rocks. Her bra is the last to go. She tosses it onto the pile as she turns to sway toward the pool beneath the falls, calling out, "Oh well, guess we'll just have to hope for the best. Maybe you can fish my ass out of the water and reattach it at the cabin later, chicken."

I laugh. "You're not going to shame me into getting into that water. No way in hell."

Her lips push into a pout as she cups her breasts in her hands. "No? What if I offer your cock a cozy place to hang out while you get used to the chill?" She presses them together, making my mouth go dry. "You could fist your hand in my hair while you fuck my breasts. That seems like a decent way to stay warm to me."

I curse and she smiles.

"You're a bad woman," I say, but I'm already shucking my t-shirt.

She giggles and spins in a circle before resuming her

sashay toward the falls. "I am. And I don't feel guilty about it at all."

In the end, I don't end up taking her up on her very generous breast-fucking offer—I love her breasts, but her pussy is too sweet to pass up. Instead, she straddles me on a smooth stone at the edge of the water, riding me hard until we're both panting and crying out loud enough to be heard over the crash of the water on the rocks below.

Once we've worked up a sweat, I let her drag me into the water up to our chests. We kiss as the falls beat down all around us and even though I'm freezing cold and pretty sure I'll never feel my balls again, the joy from this morning is still there.

Whoever gets to live the rest of his life with this woman is going to be one lucky man, and fuck...I wish it could be me.

Maybe it can, a hopeful voice whispers in my head as Binx tightens her grip on my neck, flattening her breasts against my chest. *Isn't joy a sign that you're headed in the right direction?*

Before I can think too long on that, Binx shivers against me and pulls away from our kiss with a laugh. "Oh my God, I love kissing you, but I can't handle it anymore. It's freezing in here!"

"No shit," I say, laughing as I swat her ass on the way out of the pool. "I tried to tell you, but you're a maniac."

"I *am* a maniac," she says, dashing back toward our clothes, shivering and giggling. "I can't feel my toes or my thighs or my butt!"

Twenty minutes later, we're dressed and back on the sunny side of the trail, warming up as we hike back to the four-wheeler, but we stop at the top for one last long look at the view.

Binx leans back against me, her back to my front, and I wrap her up in my arms, resting my chin on the top of her head, and it is...perfect. As perfect as every second with her since I stopped fighting the way she makes me feel.

I've spent my whole life fighting—fighting to overcome my past, to build a better future, to succeed when so many people said I would fail. But maybe it's time to lay my armor down.

Maybe it's time to soften and trust that when something feels this right, it can't be wrong.

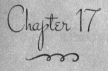

Chapter 17

BINX

If I had to pick one day to live over and over again, I'm pretty sure this would be it. I love all the memories I've made with my family and friends, and I'm so excited about starting my new career, but this time with Seven...

It's been pure magic.

Not even the appearance of Tater Tot at the edge of the porch as we're grilling sausages for dinner can mar the perfection of the past twelve hours.

"Go ahead, toss him a baby carrot from the veggie tray," Seven encourages as I position myself on the opposite side of the grill, as far from the furry potato as possible.

"Nah, I'm good," I say, taking a sip of my Chardonnay. "It's too smoky over there."

Seven shoots me an amused glance from the corners of his eyes. "Yeah? That's why you're clearing an escape route to the door?"

"I am not," I lie, even as I shift one of the deck chairs

over to make it easier for me to sprint back into the cabin, if necessary.

"He's harmless."

"That's what they all say until they come down with a bad case of groundhog cooties."

He grins, his eyes crinkling at the edges in a way I find inexplicably sexy. I love his smile lines and the hint of gray at his temples. As far as I can tell, Seven is only getting sexier with age. He's always going to be smoking hot. And if he started to soften or slow down a little, I wouldn't mind. I love his outsides, but it's his insides that turn me into a lust puddle every time he puts his arms around me.

His insides are the most beautiful thing about him.

"Groundhog cooties," he echoes, tossing a carrot to the fur potato, who chases it into the browning grass with a happy grunt. "You hear that, Tater Tot? Binx thinks you have cooties."

Tater Tot grunts again, shooting a narrow look over his shoulder that makes us both laugh, before grabbing his carrot and chowing down with enough enthusiasm to make his chubby cheeks wobble. His giant bottom teeth actually seem to get in the way for a moment, but he figures it out and resumes happily chomping and grunting.

"So, how are groundhog cooties different than normal cooties?" Seven flips the sausages, sending up a waft of delicious, spicy-scented air that makes my stomach growl.

"No idea," I say, leaning against the porch railing. "I'm too hungry to make up something entertaining. I feel like I haven't eaten in days. Must be all the fresh air."

His grin takes on a wicked lilt. "Yeah, that's probably it. Not all the calories we burned in bed this morning. Or in the bathroom or the kitchen. Or at the waterfall. At this point, I'm half dead on my feet."

I laugh, biting my lip as I shift closer, hooking a finger through his belt loop. "Poor thing. Well, don't worry. If you need an early bedtime with no extracurricular activities beforehand, I understand. Maybe we can read aloud to each other in bed, instead."

"Fuck that, reading is for nerds," he says, grabbing me around the waist and tugging me close, making me giggle as he kisses me hard.

Our teeth bump behind our lips, and I instantly decide that kissing Seven while we both laugh is also going on my list of Best Things Ever. Right along with his cock and his hands and his sexy voice in my ear and the way he smiles that new, softer smile that's just for me.

As he pulls back, gazing down at my face like he's trying to memorize every inch, I want to tell him that I love him. I want to tell him that I'd gladly take a year with him over a lifetime with anyone else.

I want to tell him that my heart is his, *forever*, even if he takes Sprout and moves a thousand miles away and never steps foot in Minnesota again.

But this isn't the time. We still have another entire day in our little paradise made for two. I don't want to ruin tomorrow by jumping the gun today.

I'll tell him everything that's in my heart, but I'll do it later, when the timing is right.

"Want to grab the buns from inside?" he murmurs, the affection in his voice making my blood buzz way more than a glass of wine ever could. "I can throw them on the grill to toast while the sausages finish up."

"Sounds good," I say. "I love a toasted bun." I slide my hand past the small of his back to grip his delicious backside through his jeans.

He grins and does the same to me. "I prefer mine covered in lace. Those panties you had on last night did things to me, McGuire. I doubt I'm ever going to get the sight of you dropping your towel by the tub out of my head."

I lift my chin, holding his gaze as I whisper, "Good. Want me to grab the salad while I'm inside, too?"

"Yeah, and the corn chips, please," he says, giving my ass a final, affectionate squeeze before setting me free. "I'm seriously starved. I don't think three sausages is going to be enough."

I laugh as I start across the porch. "You can have one of mine. Two is plenty for me, I promise." I pause with my hand on the door, sighing as Seven tosses Tater Tot another carrot. "And will you please stop feeding the rodent? I know he's your buddy, but I'd like to eat without a fur potato circling the table the entire time."

"You're a fussy woman," he teases with a mock shake of his head.

"I am," I agree. "That's why I have a pet cactus instead of an actual pet. I enjoy an orderly mealtime with no fur or teeth involved. And Mr. Prickles is always a gentleman."

Seven shakes his head. "You and that pet cactus. Sprout told me she caught you talking to it the last time she was over at your place. When you were alone and you thought she was in bed, so she knew it wasn't for her benefit."

"So?" I ask, propping a hand on my hip. "Mr. Prickles is an excellent listener. And Sprout needs to stop telling tales. What happens at Sleepover Night stays at Sleepover Night. That's the first rule of Sleepover Night. I mean, I have tales I could tell, too. Like the time she ate an entire container of whipped cream before I got up one morning, and we didn't have any for our pumpkin pie breakfast. Or the time I let her stay up until one in the morning, even though you said she had to be in bed no later than midnight."

He grunts. "I bet I can guess which sleepover night that was. Probably the one when she was a nightmare the next day. My daughter is a cranky little girl when she doesn't get at least eight hours of sleep."

I bare my teeth in a "mea culpa" grin. "Sorry. We were watching Enchanted and we couldn't stop before the happily ever after. Sprout told me stopping before the happily ever after is a proven formula for nightmares, and I couldn't give one of my favorite people nightmares. I'm not a monster."

The light in his eyes dims, and I instantly know I've said the wrong thing. "You're one of her favorites, too."

My shoulders creep toward my ears as the tension in the air builds, both of us clearly thinking of how hard this is going to be for the little girl we both love so much. "Listen, Seven, we don't have to—"

"Maybe we can figure something out," he cuts in. "A way for you two to stay close even if we..."

I press my lips together as my throat goes tight. He said "*if* we," but his face is saying "*when* we."

When we no longer see each other anymore...

Because he's still determined for this to end Friday morning. He doesn't seem to be second-guessing that decision at all, and that...hurts.

It really fucking hurts.

It hurts so badly that I can barely force myself to nod and mutter, "Yeah, sure, we'll figure it out," before hurling myself through the door into the cabin.

Once inside, I don't go to the kitchen to grab the buns and salad; I head for the bathroom and close the door, leaning back against it as I press my hands to my face. I pull in deep breaths, willing myself not to cry. I can't fall apart right now or Seven will bail on our "fuck each other's brains out for three days" plan before we've even made it all the way through day two.

He won't stay the course if he knows how badly this is hurting me, and I can't give him an excuse to push me away. Fighting for him—for us—will be a hell of a lot harder if he's sleeping on the couch and working on the cabinets all day tomorrow instead of spending time with me.

"Right, keep your eye on the ball, Binx," I say, dropping my hands to my sides and giving my reflection a hard look in the mirror. With my cheeks sun-kissed from the days outside and my lips puffy from kissing Seven an absurd number of times today, I look like a well-loved woman having the staycation of her life.

I can be that woman for another day. And then, come tomorrow night, if Seven and I are falling asleep, and he's still determined to say "so long" in the morning, maybe I'll let myself ugly cry on his chest and beg him to give us a chance.

I'm not above an ugly cry. Not even close.

I have no shame when it comes to Seven, which should probably bother me. I'm not the kind of woman who begs for a man's attention. I'm the kind who flips a man the bird and tells him to get fucked if he can't see that I'm something special.

But it's different with Seven. I *know* he thinks I'm special. It's himself that he has doubts about.

"You're going to get through to him," I tell my reflection. I stand up a little straighter, rolling my shoulders back. "He's stubborn, but he's met his match this time."

My jaw relaxes and the tension in my chest eases—because I believe it. He *has* met his match, in every way, and I'm going to make sure he realizes that by Friday morning. Look how far we've come in less than forty-eight hours. There's still time to turn this around.

Comforted by my pep talk, I head out of the bathroom and into the kitchen, arriving in time to watch a familiar car pull up the drive through the window above the sink.

Instantly, my stomach bottoms out and my heart starts beating a mile a minute.

"No," I mutter, my hands balling into fists on the counter. "No, no, no!"

I bolt for the door, planning to tell the driver to turn the hell around and leave—now! I'm fine, I'm safe, and the last thing I want is to be "rescued" from my current situation.

But by the time I reach the front of the cabin, my mother has already cut the engine and is glaring at me through the windshield of her white Kia Sorento, a mortified-looking Wendy Ann cringing in the passenger's seat beside her.

Chapter 18

SEVEN

I hear the sound of wheels on the gravel road leading up to the camp and a wave of despair hits me like a tsunami hitting shore.

No.

I'm not ready for this to be over.

I need more time. Two more nights isn't going to be enough as it is, but the thought of saying goodbye to Binx before then makes me want to lift the burning grill over my head and toss it into the yard.

Tater Tot must sense that something's wrong, because he hustles across the clearing behind the cabin and into the woods as fast as his pudgy legs will carry him, fleeing my bubbling despair. Or maybe he's just scared by the sound of the car. We don't get many vehicles up here.

I really fucking wish we weren't getting one right now, I think, then immediately feel like an asshole.

What if this is Mom coming to get me because there's a problem with Sprout? What if she had another shitty day at school, finally put chicken poop in that mean girl's

195

locker like she's been threatening to do, and got suspended or something? Or what if she climbed onto the roof again, even though I've told her a hundred times how dangerous it is, and fell off?

Fear for my daughter cutting through my selfishness, I quickly transition the sausages to a plate beside the grill and cover them with another plate to keep them warm. At least I can bring supper home with me if I'm headed back to town. Then I turn off the grill and head toward the front of the cabin, walking around the side of the building to greet the car in the driveway.

When I get there, Binx is already standing in front of a white SUV in an animated conversation with...her mother.

Oh fuck...

Her mother.

I'm sure there's someone I'd less like to see right now —an armed terrorist, maybe, or my asshole of a parole officer from back in the day—but Fran McGuire is pretty high on the list. The woman hates me. And while I can't blame her for wanting more for her daughter than an ex-con sixteen years her senior, I've also never done anything to hurt Binx. I've been a good friend to her, the kind she can count on to help clean out her gutters or change her oil for free.

I've also never crossed the line between friendship and anything more...at least not until last night.

Since then, however, I've done way more than cross the line. I've run over it in a tank, poured gasoline all over what was left of it, and set it on fire.

"Seriously, Mom, I'm fine," I hear Binx say in a

strained tone that makes me think it isn't the first time she's said the words. "I don't want to go home. It's been really nice up here, actually. Very peaceful."

"Peaceful?" her mom bleats. "Being lied to, tricked, and left in the middle of the woods with no way to call for help is *peaceful* for you? I swear, Binx, I'll never understand the way your brain works. Never, not even if I live to be a hundred and ten."

Binx sighs. "Well, obviously, but I'm okay, okay? There's no need to freak out."

"No need?" Her mom props her fists on her hips as she glares up at her taller daughter. "You could be dead! Your sister could have *killed* you."

"I'm sorry," Wendy Ann says, hanging her head out the passenger's window of the SUV. "I was just trying to be supportive and think outside the box." Fran shoots a dangerously sharp glance her way. Wendy Ann cringes lower in her seat and quickly adds, "But now I see that it was a dangerous and dumb and irresponsible thing to do. If I could go back in time, I wouldn't do it, I promise." She flaps an arm Binx's way. "But she's okay! See? We got lucky this time and everyone is fine. So, now, we can go, and I'll come back on Friday morning to get them, the way we planned."

"You'll do no such thing," Fran says, jabbing a finger at Binx. "Look at your sister. She looks like she's been through hell." She fixes her attention on her older daughter again, clutching at her neck as she shakes her head. "I swear you look like you've lost ten pounds overnight. Your face is positively haggard."

Binx's face isn't haggard. Her face is beautiful. When

we were standing by the grill and she was smiling up at me, all I could think about was how fucking perfect she is. How stunning. Her mother is clearly seeing this entire situation through fear-colored glasses.

But hopefully, I can help ease her mind.

"Hey, I thought I heard a car pull up." I force a smile as I approach from behind them, pretending I haven't been eavesdropping. "Hi, Mrs. McGuire. Wendy Ann." I nod at them in turn, ignoring the way Fran's lips pucker into a cat anus in the middle of her face in response to my appearance on the scene. I cross my arms over my chest as I come to stand beside Binx. "I just finished grilling some sausages, if you're hungry."

"We were actually just leaving," Fran says, waving Binx toward the house. "Go get your things, honey." To me she adds in a cooler voice, "I'm sorry we can't offer you a ride, too, Seven, but I have to be at my son's house for a family dinner in an hour. Wendy Ann has been in touch with your mother, however, and she said she would come get you tomorrow morning after she gets *your daughter* off to school."

The judgement in her tone on the words "your daughter" is pointed enough to tear a hole in the extra-strong denim of work jeans. Clearly, she doesn't think I should have taken time away from my parenting responsibilities to go on a fake rock-climbing trip. She has no idea that I can count the number of vacations I've taken *without* Sprout on two fingers—this trip and a white-water rafting excursion two summers ago that was too dangerous for a six-year-old—or that I'm one of the most involved parents I know.

Fran took one look at me and jumped to conclusions based on my tattoos, my motorcycle, and the fact that I'm roughly twice the size of most of the other men in town. She's not the first, and she won't be the last, and it's not like having done time does me any favors.

But I made that mistake when I was a very young man. I've been on the straight and narrow, with my head down, working hard, for two decades. I've also been devoted to raising a great kid for the past eight years, never missing a parent-teacher conference or forgetting what I promised to donate to the end-of-school potluck. Don't I ever get to put my past behind me and be judged for the things I've done right instead of the one thing I did wrong?

In a town this small?

Probably not.

Certainly not when it comes to close-minded people like Fran McGuire.

I know that, but I can't stop myself from saying, "Listen, I know this must have been scary for you. I can't imagine how I would feel if I found out my daughter had been dropped off in the woods with no way to call for help if she needed it. Even if she were in her twenties, it wouldn't matter, I'd still be scared and angry."

Fran's puckered mouth softens the slightest bit, but her gaze is still frosty.

I try again, adding, "This clearly wasn't a well-thought-out plan, and I'll be speaking to my family about their part in it when I get home to make sure they never pull a stunt like this again." I turn to Binx, smiling as I add, "But luckily, we made it to the cabin without too

199

many bumps and bruises along the way, and we've been having a wonderful time getting away from it all. Neither one of us has had a vacation in a while and this has been... really nice."

"Really, really nice," Binx murmurs, but before our little love fest can get too cozy, Fran cuts in.

"Speaking of vacation," she says, her tone hot and sharp. "I don't know why you thought now was a good time to take an entire week off work, Binx. The housing market is crazy right now. Aren't you worried your clients will feel abandoned? I'm sure at least one of them is closing this week, and think of all the new business you're missing out on by not being at your desk. My friend Kim's daughter is starting her house hunt this weekend, and I told her to call you about getting pre-approved."

Fran exhales a long-suffering sigh. "Now, I'll have to call her back, and tell her to try you when you're at your desk next week. Unless you plan on heading back into the bank tomorrow. I'm sure it's not too late to get your vacation days reinstated if you want to go in. Albie is the sweetest boss in the world. He's always so good about working with you. And if you go in this week, you'll have more time to take off for the holidays. Everyone's going to be here this year. All the cousins are flying in from Texas, and Tatum's entire family is going to be here from Kentucky. She has nearly as many siblings as you do, so we're going to need all-hands-on-deck to find beds for them and keep everyone entertained."

"I'm happy to host one of Tatum's sisters at my house," Binx says, "they sound great, but..."

"But what?" Fran huffs again and glances at the slim

gold watch on her wrist. "We should talk about this on the way back into town. Go grab your things. I'll open the tailgate and you can just throw the entire mess in and sort through it later. If we don't go soon, we're going to be late."

"Mom, I'm not going with you," Binx says, standing firm. "And I'm not taking time off from the bank. I quit."

Oh, shit...

Apparently, she's decided it's time to take a stand with her mother, which I fully support, but I can't help wishing she'd done it at a later date, when I wasn't present. Fran is a proud woman, who thinks she knows what's best for her children. The only thing harder than having her daughter defy her is having that defiance witnessed by a stranger.

As I could have predicted, Fran's eyes widen and shift straight to me, accusation flaring in her gaze before she glances back to Binx. "What? You quit? Why on earth did you quit? You're doing so well there. You're one of their top loan officers."

"I quit because I hated my job, Mom," Binx says, her shoulders hitching closer to her ears.

Fran emits a startled squawk. "What? But you always looked happy when I stopped by the bank. And Albie adores you."

"I like Albie, too," Binx says, "and all the other people I worked with. It wasn't the people. It was the job. I don't want to be a loan officer. I never did." She drags a clawed hand through her hair before adding, "Hell, I didn't even want to go to business school. I just couldn't think of anything I actually wanted to do that wouldn't make you disappointed in me. But I've realized there's something more important than you being disappointed in me, Mom. There's *me* being disappointed in me, and that's how I've felt lately. I've felt like a coward, too chickenshit to do what I really want with my life. But it's *my* life, and I have to live it the way that feels right to me, not to anyone else."

Fran's jaw hangs open for a beat before she sputters, "Well, I... I never said you had to major in business. I never even said you had to go to college. When you talked about going to trade school to learn welding, I wasn't happy about how dangerous that can be, but I was open to it. We discussed it."

Binx shoulders lift and lower, but I don't hear her breathe. "Yeah, I know. But I didn't want to learn how to weld because I wanted to be a welder on a construction site, Mom. I wanted to be a welder because I wanted to scavenge scrap metal from the junkyard and make sculptures out of it like this amazing artist I was following on social media at the time." Her fingers dig into her waist through the black thermal she put on after our shower. "But I knew if I told you that, you'd think I was insane, so business school seemed like the easier choice. I thought I'd be okay with a job I didn't love as long as I had time to pursue my hobbies in my free time, but I'm not."

Fran crosses her arms and shoots me another "why are you here?" look before turning back to Binx.

But I can't go inside. I can't leave Binx to fight this battle alone, even if I'm just here as silent moral support.

I know how hard this is for her, how long she's wanted to stand up to her mother but felt like she couldn't make waves. No one makes waves with Fran. She's the matriarch of the McGuire clan and not even Barrett, the most abrasive McGuire sibling, dares to cross her. When Fran tells him to jump, he asks how high, just like the rest of them.

Seeing how Fran bullies her kids has made me even more grateful for the respectful support my mother has always given me. She makes her opinion known on everything from what I'm doing with my business to whether or not Sprout is allowed to go swimming if she hasn't finished her reading for the day, but in the end, she respects my decisions. Even if they're different than hers.

Fran proves, yet again, that she's not about that respectful kind of parenting when she says, "So, what are you going to do? Just...hang around in the woods until you find yourself? Because finding yourself won't pay the bills, Binx. And you're not a young woman anymore."

"I'm twenty-six, Mom," Binx says, her cheeks flushing bright red.

"Nearly twenty-seven, in just a couple weeks," her mother corrects. "I was married and had three children by the time I was your age. Three! The time for finding your-self is over. This is the time when you buckle down and work hard to build an adult life."

"I have an adult life," Binx shoots back, her tone heat-ing, as well. "Just because it looks different than yours, doesn't mean it's not worthy of respect. I'm sick of everyone in this family acting like the only way to be a full-fledged grown-up is to get married and have kids. I don't know if I even want to have biological kids. Does that mean I'm always going to be treated like a fucking child?"

"Beatrice Anna McGuire, don't you dare curse at me," Fran says, clutching her imaginary pearls in earnest now. Her knuckles are white at the neck of her sweater.

"Guys, please," Wendy Ann pleads from the passenger's window, casting me a glance that's both apologetic and pleading. It's clear she wants me to intervene, but I already know nothing I say is going to make this better. "Let's not do this right now. Tatum's making prime rib, Mom. You love her prime rib, let's just go and—"

"Quiet, Wendy Ann," her mother snaps. "I don't know what's gotten into you, Binx. Or who..." She cuts a chilling glance my way that makes my balls inch higher, seeking shelter from the cold. "But you were raised better than this. You're embarrassing me. And yourself."

Binx emits a humorless laugh. "There it is. That's all you really care about. How things look and whether the way I live my life reflects badly on *you*."

"That's not true," Fran says. "I never—"

"Well, I'm sorry, Mom," Binx says, her eyes glittering as she barrels on, "but I don't care about that anymore. I never have. I'm sick of pretending I share your values. I don't. I actually think a lot of your values are just as messed up as you do mine. So, we'll just have to make peace with that and try to love each other anyway, because I'm done trying to be anyone but who I am. I start full time at the tattoo parlor next week. I'm going to be a tattoo artist."

Fran emits a strangled yip of alarm, but Binx isn't done yet. I know that—I can feel the unfinished business heavy in the air as she pulls in her next breath—but her next words still shock the shit out of me.

"And I'm going to be in love with this man." She shifts her focus, pinning me with a look so raw and real, it connects like a fist to the gut. "I'm going to be in love with him for the rest of my life, whether he gets on board with loving me back or not. He's the one for me. Just him. No one else." She sucks in a breath, her brow furrowing. "So...there's that. I'm sorry, Seven. I know I said I was fine with a fling before we went our separate ways, but I lied. I'm not okay with it. I want more. I want it all."

She takes a step toward me, turning her back on her mother and sister, "I want to share my life with you and help raise Sprout and be a family. I want to spend every night with you and wake up next to you every morning, and I don't give a shit that you're older than I am. I honestly couldn't care less." She shakes her head, her eyes shining. "It doesn't fucking matter. What matters is that I've never felt this way before, not with anyone else in the world. You make me feel so beautiful and smart and funny and...enough. More than enough. Just the way I am." Her gaze searches mine. "I think I make you feel the same way. And if I do...isn't that worth fighting for?"

Wendy Ann emits a soft "come on, man, say the right thing," sound from the passenger's seat, but my focus doesn't waiver from Binx's face.

She has me locked in, completely captivated. I'm not sure if we're in the final scene of a romantic movie or in the middle of a slow-motion car crash, but I couldn't look away if I tried.

She's right, I *do* feel all those things.

I love her. I adore her. I want her to be my family more than I've wanted anything in a very long time...

But she has no idea how much harder things get as you age. Life piles on. It piles on and piles on, one crisis after another, until getting up after you've been knocked down becomes a Herculean task.

By the fifth or sixth or seventeenth time you've dragged yourself back to your feet, you're getting up with kneecaps shattered by grief and the weight of a broken system strapped to your back. And sure, you keep going —you have a kid to raise, a family to support—but it's soul crushing.

Everything inside you is screaming that it shouldn't be this hard. That there should be more goodness in the world, more mercy, more forgiveness...

But there isn't.

And avoiding pain becomes so much easier than reaching for pleasure...

I haven't always been like this. I used to believe that I could trust my heart, my gut, to lead me to the person who was right for me. But that was before I failed my wife, before she died, before I dated half a dozen different women over the years and every relationship ended in disaster. Sometimes it was my fault, sometimes it was theirs, but no matter how many times I've tried, romance always ends in disappointment and pain.

I've had enough pain, and I've really had enough of hurting people.

The tears in Binx's eyes are killing me.

Yes, it will tear her apart if I walk away, but in the

long run it will be far less painful than if we roll the dice and fail. She's still so young. She still has hope. She'll find someone else, someone better, less jaded, more open to life and love and becoming the kind of partner she needs.

For a moment there, I thought maybe I could be that man, but that was just my selfish side wanting to keep Binx in my life.

She deserves more. Her mother knows it, and *I* know it. I'm not enough for her, and the only way to prove I'm not the shit human being half the town thinks I am is to end this with a clean break. Right now.

So, I call on the skills I've acquired throughout a lifetime of dealing with cruel people and crueler twists of fate. I drag the soft part of me into a vault deep inside and lock it away. I snap the cord connecting my heart to the rest of me and say in a voice so calm it's a little shocking, even to me, "I'm sorry, sweetheart, but we're not on the same page. You should go with your mother. I'll give you privacy to collect your things."

Then I turn and walk away, headed back toward the shed at the rear of the property and the four-wheeler. There's still a little gas left in the tank, enough to get me out of earshot for the next hour or however long it takes Binx to finish screaming or crying or cursing my name— whatever she has to do to work through her feelings and realize it's time to leave.

But as I reach the shed and push inside, I don't hear so much as a peep from behind me. Binx doesn't call my name, she doesn't cry, she doesn't tell me I'm a pathetic, cowardly liar. There's nothing, not so much as an outraged huff from her mom or a plea to come back and play nice from Wendy Ann.

As I rev the engine and pull through the open door, I risk a glance their way, just to make sure they're all still standing, but no one is paying me any attention. Fran is already behind the wheel, checking her lipstick in the visor mirror, Wendy Ann is slumped low in the passenger's seat, and Binx is nowhere to be seen.

She must already be inside, gathering her bag, which is...good.

It's *good* that she instantly knew to take me at my word, that she realized continuing to fight for me was a losing game and popped right inside to grab her things. I'm truly glad she's sparing us both a bigger scene.

I also feel like absolute shit.

Like garbage.

Like something even less desirable than garbage.

Nuclear waste, maybe...

That's a fitting comparison. I'm toxic, dangerous. I always have been and I always will be. That's why I should spend the rest of my life alone, focused on raising my child to be a good person who knows how to have functional relationships. I'm not going to make anyone's romantic dreams come true, but Sprout might one day. She's an incredible kid and has so much love in her heart.

And a lot of that love is for Binx, the caustic voice in my head rasps as I head up the trail into the woods. *She's going to hate you for fucking this up. She might never forgive you.*

Maybe the voice is right, but I can't worry about that right now. I made the only decision that I could live with.

If I'd done anything else, I wouldn't have been able to forgive myself.

Holding tight to that thought and ignoring the other voice, the one in my gut screaming that I have to turn around now, before it's too late, I punch the accelerator, sending leaves flying into the air as I zoom over the hill and the cabin disappears behind me.

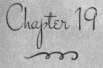

Chapter 19

SEVEN

I park the four-wheeler at the small pond where Sprout likes to fish and sit staring at the bugs swarming above the golden water for over an hour. There aren't many days like this left in the year. Soon, the sun will be setting hours earlier, over a sheet of ice surrounded by snow drifts.

Sprout's so excited for skating season. I promised I would bring her up as soon as the ice was thick enough, and we'd spend the entire afternoon on the pond. I already have everything I need to make a little warming hut for her as a surprise. I figured I could put a firepit in there, our old futon, and supplies for making hot chocolate, so we could really make a day of it.

But in my mind, Binx was always here with us.

She's a phenomenal skater. Last year she took Sprout with her to watch the intramural hockey tournament Binx plays in with her brothers. Sprout couldn't stop talking about it after. She doesn't want to be a figure skater girl anymore, she wants to be strong and fast, like Binx.

I hate that I've taken someone she loves so much away from my daughter.

I hate the black hole in my gut that feels like it's sucking all the misery in the world deep inside it.

I hate that I have to go back to the cabin and sleep alone in the bed I shared with Binx, the one where the sheets still smell like her.

It makes me wish I'd razed the cabin to the ground, after all. It had mold in the walls and foundation issues that took months to get sorted out before I could even start the renovation. It wouldn't have cost much more to demolish and start with a fresh slate, but the cabin is nearly a hundred years old. I wanted to help preserve the history of the camp, while building additional facilities to attract new people to the land.

Now I think—fuck history.

I wish I could erase the history of the past two days from my mind. I wish I had no idea how good it feels to touch her, kiss her, hold her close as she falls asleep and feel like I have everything I need right there in my arms.

I was at peace with her, but it was a stolen peace, a rotten one.

"It's your fault," I mutter to my dick as I relieve myself against a tree. "You're a weak-willed piece of shit."

It has the decency to look ashamed of itself as I tuck it back in my pants, but shame isn't going to do either one of us any good.

That's what I always tell Sprout—don't let shame

take root inside you. It's okay to feel bad about something you did; it's not okay to feel like *you're* the bad thing. That kind of thinking only dulls your light, hurts your heart, and makes it harder to be the good person you want to be.

It's hard to love other people right if you don't love yourself.

I know that to be true with every piece of me. I also know that it's way easier said than done, especially when you're a middle-aged man who's made so many mistakes. I thought I'd have more things figured out by now, but all I really know is that I'll never understand other people. I'll be lucky if, some day, I reach a place where I truly know myself.

Trying not to think about the memories I wish Binx could have made with us here this winter, I get back on the four-wheeler and head toward the cabin. I've been gone nearly two hours by the time I pull into the shed, long enough for the sun to set and soft pink light to fill the air.

There's a chill in the air, too, the cold cutting through my shirt as I head toward the porch, intending to snag the plate of sausages I left outside and force myself to eat something.

But when I reach the grill, the plates and the veggie tray are gone. For a second, I wonder if Tater Tot somehow found his way up onto the grill and made off with all the food, but there's no sign of a smashed plate on the ground. And Tater Tot is surprisingly agile, but he's also bulked up for winter. I don't know if he'd be capable of climbing the grill at this point, which is a good thing. Eating a bunch of processed meat would have made him sick if he'd tried it.

As soon as I dismiss that theory, I realize what must have happened.

Binx cleaned up before she left.

Instantly, I feel even worse than I did before. I broke her heart and in return, she cleaned up my mess. Or maybe she took the sausages with her as some small form of retribution.

I hope so. I hope she took all the food in the house and left me to forage for acorns with the groundhogs. It's what I deserve...better than I deserve.

With a sigh, I double-check again to make sure the propane is turned off on the grill, then plod inside, trying to think of what to listen to on the speaker that might take my mind off my abject misery. Maybe that podcast about people getting murdered in national parks. Those people had it much worse than I'm having it right now.

Maybe I'll manage to unsettle myself enough that going to sleep in the middle of the woods alone with no way out will start to feel scary. Better to lie awake in bed, fearful of being axe-murdered, than lie awake thinking about Binx.

"Binx." Her name bursts from my lips without my permission when I close the door and turn to see her sitting on the couch in the living room, surrounded by pieces of paper from the notepad I use to make lists for the hardware store. She's bent over the pad now, writing furiously, the tip of her tongue sticking out between her lips as she concentrates.

"Yep. It's me. I'm still here." She doesn't so much as

glance up from her scribbling as she adds, "You didn't actually think I would leave, did you?"

The dinosaur jaws locked around my chest loosen, and I draw my first deep breath since I saw her mother standing in front of the cabin.

No, I realize, I didn't actually think she would leave. Maybe that's part of the reason I felt like such absolute shit when I thought she had.

"I'm sorry," I say, knowing there's so much more that needs to be said, but I'm just so grateful to see her sitting there, looking absolutely unconcerned with the future, that I can't think straight.

"You should be," she says, still writing. "That was mortifying. It's hard enough to have your profession of love dismissed without having your family there to watch it happen. Especially my mom. She practically had kittens when I told her I was staying to talk to you, and that if she wanted me to leave, she would have to physically over-power me and tie me up in the back of her SUV." She dots a period onto the paper and finally looks up, her eyes pink from crying, but now dry and clear. "I think she thought about it for a second or two, but then she remembered I'm not four years old anymore. She can't just pick me up and carry me away from things I love, kicking and screaming."

"I didn't mean to hurt you," I say. "I never did."

"But you did," she says calmly, the complete lack of blame in her tone somehow making me feel even worse. "You really, really hurt me, and I think I know why. It's not because you're dead set against getting involved with someone so much younger than you are."

I arch a brow, but don't speak. Words are still elusive. I'm too lost in the emotions slamming against my chest like ocean waves on a stormy day. Fear, grief, gratitude, guilt, misery—they slam into me over and over again, while high above the shoreline, a single seagull cries out not to lose hope.

But that's the problem. I don't have enough hope to make it through all the challenges Binx and I would face as a couple. The world has beaten the hope out of me.

I'm about to tell her as much when she says, "You don't think you're good enough for me," and my next breath gets stuck in my lungs.

I hold it for a long beat, then exhale in a rush, back to not knowing what to say.

She's right, but she's also wrong. I'm *not* good enough, but not because I'm a bad man. I just...

"I'm just so fucking tired, baby," I say my voice rough.

She frowns. "No, you're not. You're the strongest man I know. You run at least five miles a day and could bench press a Volkswagen."

"I don't mean that kind of tired." I move into the kitchen, bracing my hands on the island, facing her across it. "I don't believe in happy endings anymore. The world isn't happy and neither are most of the people in it. That doesn't mean they're bad or that I'm bad, it just...is what it is. I've come to accept that and be mostly okay with it. But learning to be okay with it..." I trail off, my shoulders inching closer to my ears as I drop my gaze to the counter. "I don't know. I think it killed the part of me that believed I could make love work for the long haul."

"You love Sprout and your mom," she says. "And your brothers and your nephews."

"It's different."

"How?" she asks.

I look up, meeting her still calm gaze. At least she's taking this well. But, of course she is. She's the strongest person *I* know—male or female. "They're family."

"Which means," she presses.

"They're family, they're...forever," I say, with a soft huff of laughter. "I couldn't get rid of them if I tried."

"You can't get rid of me, either," she says, arching a brow. "I'm still here. I'm not going to leave you, if that's what you're worried about."

"I'm not—" I break off, the words feeling like a lie in my mouth.

But I'm *not* worried that she's going to leave me.

Am I?

"I'm not going to leave, even if things get hard," she continues. "Even if you get old, and I'm not quite as old just yet. Even if you grow a giant wart on your shoulder that makes your clothes fit funny and you aren't as hot as you were before."

"A wart could always be removed," I say, addressing the easy part of all that.

"Okay, then it's not a wart. It's a hematoma, and it's all tangled up with your nervous system. They can't remove it or you'll be paralyzed from the neck down, so you have to keep it. Right there on your shoulder, huge and gross, like a creepy, puss-filled second head."

My upper lip curls. "Gross."

"Damn straight," she agrees, uncrossing her legs and

rising to her feet. "It would be disgusting, but it wouldn't make me leave you. I'd draw a smiley face on it, name it Athena, and kiss it goodnight when we got into bed."

My nose wrinkles along with my lip. "I don't want that for you. Or me."

"Well, tough shit. That's what you're getting. Turns out, I'm even more loyal than I thought. Once I fall in love, that's it. There's no undoing it." She reaches down, gathering several of the sheets of paper from the couch and coffee table in front of her. "That's why I made you a list."

I arch a brow. "A list?"

"Yes, a list of all the reasons *I'm* not good enough for you," she says, rifling through them until she finds what she's looking for. "Number one, when I was a freshman in high school, I cheated on all my history quizzes. My friend, Wendell, would tip his paper so I could see his choices, and I blatantly copied and took my B+ like I deserved it. And I didn't thank him for the help nearly as much as I should have."

My lips twitch. "Terrible."

"I know. But don't worry, it gets worse," she agrees, tossing the first sheet into the air. As it flutters to the ground, she reads from the second one, "When I was five and Wendy Ann was two, I carried her up to the treehouse and left her there. Because I was annoyed with her for always following me around, and I knew she couldn't get down on her own. And yes, I was pretty sure, at five, that she was too much of a scaredy cat to try the ladder, but I could have been wrong. I could have killed my little sister."

"You were five," I say. "It wasn't your responsibility to keep your little sister safe. Someone should have been watching Wendy Ann. And you. An adult. I never left Sprout alone outside unsupervised until last summer, and even then, only for a little while."

Binx's lips hook into a humorless grin. "Yeah, well, that's not how the McGuires did things. I'm sure one of my brothers was supposed to be watching us, but went to go play basketball instead. We had too many kids for Mom to keep up with all of us, and Dad was at the store working most of the time."

"So, I'm a better parent than your mother?" I tease. "Is that what you're saying?"

Her brow furrows even as her gaze softens. "Yes! So much better. Don't you dare let her get into your head about taking a few days away from Sprout. Parents need vacations and time away from their kids. There's nothing wrong with that. It's healthy for everyone."

"I know," I say. "But she's not wrong about everything. I have a reputation in this town. Whether it's deserved or not doesn't really matter. I'm always going to be defined by my mistakes, and if you were with me, you would be, too."

"I don't care," she says without a beat of hesitation. "Not even a little bit. You know why? Because I've done way worse things than drive a getaway car. I just didn't get caught." She pulls in a breath and her throat works as she swallows, making me think this is a more serious confession than the other two. "But I've never told this to anyone. Never. I don't even like to think about it in my own head. Every time the memory comes up, I shove it way down and pretend it didn't happen. But it did and... if people in Bad Dog knew, if my family knew, they would think *I* was the bad influence."

I nod slowly, my brows inching closer together as I study her face. She's pale and there's sweat breaking out on her lip despite the chill in the cabin. "You don't have to tell me," I assure her. "We all have things we're ashamed of that we keep to ourselves. That's totally normal."

She gives a quick shake of her head. "No. I want to. I'm going to. I just..." She swallows again. "I just need you to turn around. I can't say it to your face, but I'm pretty sure I can say it to your back." I start to protest, but she breaks in, "Please, just...turn around. You owe me that much for bailing on me outside with Mom and Wendy Ann."

"I owe you at least one," I agree, but I hesitate again. I don't want her to do this. I seriously doubt anything she has to say is going to make me think any less of her, but this is obviously painful, and the last thing I want to do is cause her more pain. "I hate to see you hurting," I finally say.

Her lips twitch, though her eyes remain haunted. "That's why you've got to turn around, dude. Do it. I want to do this. I *need* to do it."

My tongue slips out to wet my lips. I want to keep fighting her, but she has that determined look in her eye, the one I know makes her nearly unstoppable. So finally, with one final sigh, I turn around, lean back against the counter with my arms crossed, and brace for whatever is about to happen.

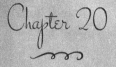

Chapter 20

BINX

It can't be more than sixty degrees in the cabin—I was so distracted by scribbling down my darkest confessions that I let the fire in the woodstove go out—but I'm sweating.

Beads of sweat form on my lip and the hollow of my spine is sticky beneath my shirt. Meanwhile, my heart is beating in my stomach, and I can't seem to pull in a full breath.

I've never said what I'm about to say out loud.

Even writing it down made me feel sick.

But I want to do this. I want Seven to know, without a doubt, that he isn't alone in having done things he's not proud of. Hopefully, that will make him feel better about himself moving forward, even if he decides I'm a monster he doesn't want anywhere near his family.

"So, I..." I start, my voice breaking on the second word. I pause, clear my throat, swallow, and will myself to get this done as quickly as possible. "I'm just going to read what I wrote," I say, directing my focus to the page in my hand. "It'll be easier that way."

"All right," Seven rumbles, his broad back still turned to me. But I can hear the compassion in his voice, and it makes me even more anxious. I don't deserve compassion, not for this, anyway.

"My grandmother was one of my favorite people," I read, grateful it *does* seem to be easier to read than to speak off the top of my head. Still, just saying the word "grandmother" sends pain spreading through my chest. It always does. "She was unconventional for a woman, especially for her time. She loved to tinker with machines. Toasters, washing machines, cars—you name it, she could fix it. She helped my grandad run his auto body shop and had a side hustle fixing appliances. In another time, she probably would have been an engineer or something, but she grew up in a super traditional Catholic household in the fifties. Girls were supposed to get married and have babies, or maybe teach school or go into nursing, that was it. She was the first person to tell me I didn't have to play by the rules. If I didn't want to go to church, I didn't have to. If I wanted to wear my brothers' old clothes and play sports and cut my hair short, I could. She always pushed back against my mother when she tried to force me into fluffy Easter dresses and pink tennis shoes."

"Sounds like a badass lady," Seven says.

I nod, even though he can't see me. "She was. But she was also so kind and compassionate. She always reminded me that my mother had been longing to have little girls through the birth of all my big, stinky brothers. She helped me see that my mother wasn't doing these things to torment me and Mel and Wendy Ann. It was just that she had a dream that didn't quite match up with reality. Dreams are hard to let go of, even when two of your daughters are tomboys and one of them finds blocks and robots way more fascinating than ballet or baby dolls."

Seven grunts and my lips flicker up.

"Yeah, I know you're not Mom's biggest fan," I say. "I don't blame you. I'm not very happy with her right now, either."

"You're a wonderful person and daughter," Seven says. "It's crazy to me that she can't see that. It hurts to see her hurt you."

My brow furrows and the back of my nose starts to sting. "Thanks, but..." I suck in a breath and exhale in a rush, "But we'll see what you think of me after I'm finished with this." He starts to speak, but I cut him off, "Please, just let me finish. I'm at the hard part, and I really just want to get it out and then burn this piece of paper."

"Okay," he murmurs, before falling silent again.

I take another bracing breath before I continue, "Gran was my cheerleader and my teacher and one of my best friends. I don't know if I would have had the courage to become the person I wanted to be without her. When she got cancer when I was a junior in high school, I was devastated. I quit the softball team so I could spend more time with her after school. I'd take her to chemo and bring her home again. We'd watch movies and go through her old photo albums and just...shoot the shit for hours. Sometimes, other family members would come over to hang out, too, but it was mostly me and Gran."

I press my lips together, fighting for control, and

continue in an only slightly wobbly voice, "When the first round of chemo didn't work, and she relapsed a year later, I was the one who fought to help her keep living at home, even though she was so weak. But she didn't want to move in with my parents or have a nurse with her all the time. She was a private, independent person."

"Sounds familiar," Seven murmurs.

"Thanks," I say, willing myself not to cry. If I cry, it will only make this take longer, and I'm so ready to be done with it. "While she was waiting to start chemo again, we took turns staying with her. One night, my mom had been on duty all afternoon and was positive Gran was taking a turn for the worse. She made me promise to call for an ambulance if I heard her gasping for air the way she had several times earlier that day. I said I would, but a few hours later, when Gran started having trouble breathing again..." I curl my free hand into a fist, my nails biting into my palm as my heart punches at my ribs. "I didn't call the ambulance. I did what she asked me to do. She said she was done fighting. She was ready to go, so I ..." I bite my bottom lip, horror swelling inside of me like a poisonous balloon about to pop. But this is the truth, and it's high time I told it. "I let her go. I stood there and just...watched while she died."

A sob escapes my lips, but before I can reach for a tissue or press the heels of my hands to my eyes to stop the tears, Seven is somehow in front of me. I don't remember seeing him move. One second, he's on the other side of the island, with his back turned to me; the next, he's dragging me against his chest and holding me so tight, I can barely breathe.

"Oh, sweetheart," he says, the love in his voice making me feel even worse.

I try to squirm free, but he's got me in a lock. "I'm not a sweetheart, I'm a murderer," I sob against his hard chest.

"No, you're not. You're the badass she raised you to be," he says. "You honored her wishes, even though what she asked was way too much to put on a seventeen-year-old kid."

"I was eighteen," I say, curling my fingers into the soft fabric of his shirt. "I was about to graduate."

"Same difference. You were a kid," he says. "But you were probably the only person in her life with a heart big and brave enough to let her go with dignity."

My face crumples again. "It wasn't dignified. It was awful. She gasped and writhed on the bed. It was...horrific." I shudder and Seven hugs me even harder.

"That was just biology, a body fighting to live even though the spirit was ready to go. That's just how humans are wired. I promise you that she was so proud of you. You did the right thing."

I fight to swallow past the fist shoving up my throat. "I don't know," I rasp. "I've always wondered if she ch-changed her mind at the last minute. If she died hating me for being a monster."

"Never," he says without a beat of hesitation. "She loved you. And she was what, seventy? Eighty?"

"Eighty-two," I mumble. "She didn't have Mom until she was thirty something. It was late for back then."

"Eighty-two years is plenty of time to know your own mind," he says. "And it sounds like she knew hers better than most. She wouldn't have asked you to do what you did without a lot of thought. She knew what she wanted." He pulls back, gazing down at me. "Don't doubt that. She wouldn't want you to. You saved her from a life that was causing her nothing but suffering. You were her hero."

Fresh tears stream down my cheeks. "I loved her so much. I couldn't say no. She'd already asked me twice before that week not to call the ambulance if she started to go. She'd decided she didn't want to go back to the hospital or try chemo again. She said she was r-ready."

He brushes his palm over my forehead, smoothing my hair back. "And she was. It's time to let this go. You aren't a murderer. You're a brave woman who did a very hard thing to help someone you loved. Like you always do."

I sniff. "This isn't why I told you. I didn't want you to comfort me or...absolve me or whatever. I wanted you to know that I have crazy shit in my past, too. If anything, I'm not good enough for you, not vice versa."

He shakes his head, the love in his eyes unwavering. "Nope. Not even close. You're one in a million. One in a hundred million. The world doesn't deserve you."

"That's not true," I say. "At least half the people I know think I'm too much. Too loud or too bossy or just...weird."

He cups my face in his big hand, making me feel tiny the way only he can. "Courage can seem weird in a world full of cowards. I'm sorry I was one of them."

"Was?" I squeak, a tiny flicker of hope sparking to life inside my chest. "Does that mean you're not going to be one anymore?"

"I'm going to try," he says. "And when I fail, I trust you'll let me know it's time to step up my game."

Another sob spasms in my chest, but this one is all relief. "Really?"

He nods, his brow furrowing as he brushes his thumb across my jaw. "When I was driving around before, after I thought you'd left, I kept thinking that I was too broken for you. That I didn't have the hope for the future that younger people have. That I was too beaten down by life to be good for you. But now I'm starting to think maybe that's a good thing."

I frown. "I don't understand."

His lips press together for a beat before he adds in a slower voice, "I know how cruel the world can be. I've had enough experience by now that a lot of the time, I can see it coming, and shift direction before it can knock me flat. I was so busy thinking of all the ways that loving you could knock me flat, I didn't stop to think about the other side of this."

My brows pinch closer together as I give another little shake of my head, still not certain where he's going with this.

His lips curve. "I can use my experience with getting body slammed by life to keep it from body slamming the woman I love. I can keep you safe from the things that tried to take my hope away. Maybe not all of them, but at least some. And maybe I can keep them from taking yours."

Heart melting, I wrap my arms around his waist. "I don't need you to protect me, Seven. I just need you to love me back."

"Well, tough shit, McGuire," he rumbles. "Protection is one of the services I provide. It's just the way I'm built."

"I like the way you're built," I whisper, leaning into him, until my breasts are flattened against his chest. "I'm going to like it forever, even if you turn into a shriveled old man who needs me to carry him up the rock face on my back in a sling."

He smiles, a soft, loving, trusting smile I want to keep on his face forever. "Hopefully, it won't come to that, but thanks. In the meantime, I'll do my damnedest to stay in peak physical condition, so I can keep up with my sexy younger girlfriend."

I couldn't fight the smile bursting across my face if I tried. "Girlfriend. I like the sound of that."

"Me, too," he says, his eyes shining. "I love you, Binx. I'm really glad you didn't give up on me."

"Never," I promise. "Now help me burn my sins and take me to bed."

"Done," he vows, and he's a man of his word.

We stoke the fire back to life and toss all my scribbles on the flames. Then he picks me up and carries me to bed, where we make love with a sweet, wild abandon that makes me feel closer to a person than I ever have before. When he comes inside me, crying my name, I wrap every limb around him, holding him close, never wanting to forget a second of this—the first night of our forever.

"Forever," I murmur, kissing his shoulder. "I'm going to keep you forever."

"Not if I keep you first," he says, lifting his head to smile down at me. "How would you feel about cold sausages in bed?"

I shake my head. "Nah, I like my sausages hot." I wiggle beneath him, humming happily at the feel of his cock still buried inside me.

He laughs. "Thanks, but seriously, I'm starving. Despair followed by hot sex makes me hungry."

I nod. "Me, too. Let's go eat all the things."

So, we do. Then we turn on the speaker and dance to a John Denver song Seven says reminds him of me, and I cry a little.

But it's a happy cry.

I'm so happy, nothing can bring me down.

Not even arriving home Friday morning to find a five-page letter from my mother detailing all the ways I've let her down.

I simply burn the letter—very therapeutic, would highly recommend—and leave her a voicemail saying, "I love you, Mom, but I meant what I said at the cabin. I'm living my life in my integrity now, not yours. Also, Seven and I are a couple. I'm in love and so happy. I would love for you to be happy for me, but if you can't, that's okay, too. Keeping your lips zipped is an excellent second choice."

I end the message with a sigh and tell Mr. Prickles, "Yeah, I know. It's not nearly as hard as I thought it would be. I should have stood up to her years ago."

Mr. Prickles agrees.

Then, he has a few choice words to speak of his own

on the subject of the fur potato currently making himself at home in our space.

"I know, I know," I say, watching Tater Tot tear apart one of the old dog toys Keanu Reeves left here the last time he slept over. "But turns out his bottom teeth need to be filed by humans."

It's some kind of birth defect, and that's why they stick out so much. We noticed Tater Tot really starting to struggle to eat even apple slices by our last day there. It was like his lips were getting tangled up in his own teeth or something.

Seven called a vet friend of his to ask about it once Wendy Ann returned with our cell phones. He came out to do an exam and in just a few minutes delivered the news that Tater Tot was never going to be able to live successfully in the wild long term. Then, the vet said he would fast track my application to be on his animal rescue team, so I could legally keep the fur potato as a pet, so...

"He's a sweetheart, really," I add to my cranky cactus. "I promise. He'll grow on you. Like a sweet, grunty fungus."

Mr. Prickles shoots me a sharply needled look.

I lift my hands in the air. "I know, I hate rodents, too, but...look at him. He's precious. And he's had his shots and the vet filed his teeth. He's at least fifty percent less creepy looking than he was before, and Seven promised to shift him over to living at his place as soon as we see if he's comfortable around the chickens."

Mr. Prickles rolls his spines and mutters something about poultry being for eating, not cuddling.

"Oh, come on, don't be that way. You know Sprout loves her chickens." I pick him up, cooing closer to his pokey little cactus belly. "And I love you. We're going to find a way to blend into one big, happy family. I promise."

And...we do.

There months later, I'm fully moved in with my new family at Seven's place, where I intend to stay for the next hundred years.

Or however long the universe gives me.

No matter how long it is, I already know it won't be long enough.

Epilogue

Wendy Ann McGuire

*The last single McGuire sibling standing.
(Or rather, running, away from her mother's
matchmaking as fast as her spindly
nerd legs can carry her...)*

"All those tattoos. I'll never understand it." Mom sighs and shakes her head, but there's a smile tugging at her lips as she adds, "Though they looked nice with the flowers she chose for the bouquet."

"They looked amazing," I agree as Seven spins my sister around the floor for their first dance. "*She* looks amazing."

Binx is gorgeous in a form-fitting white satin gown

and fancy up-do, but it's the expression on her face as she gazes up at Seven that makes her shine.

She's so in love, so happy...and I can't help feeling smug about it.

After all, if Sprout, Seven's eight-year-old daughter, and I hadn't parent-trapped these two, this wedding might never have happened. I catch Sprout's eye across the ballroom and grin, shooting her a subtle thumbs-up. She grins and gives me two enthusiastic thumbs-up back as she sways to the music, clearly ready for the first song to be over so we can join the lovebirds on the dance floor.

"My baby girl," Mom says, dabbing at the corners of her eyes. "All grown up and married and starting a family of her own." She pats my arm with a sniff. "That just leaves you, sweetheart. Which reminds me, Petey Sinclair is here. Remember Petey? From when you were little?"

My smile falls from my face.

Maybe if I pretend that I didn't hear her, she'll let it go.

"You know, Petey Sinclair," she adds, proving she's still my mother and not about to let anything go. Ever. "You used to play in his sandbox when you were little, and his mother and I were still doing those Tupperware parties. You had so much fun together. You'd be out there digging for hours."

"No, I don't remember," I say, though I do. I remember Petey Sinclair being a pain in the butt who hogged the good shovel and kept insisting I play with his wrestler dolls, even though I have always had the good sense—even at five years old—to hate wrestling.

Mom huffs. "I find that hard to believe. You played together all the time."

"I was five, Mom," I mutter.

"So?" She lifts a hand to fluff her immaculate bob. I don't know how she gets her hair to behave so well, but it's not a trait I inherited. Fifteen minutes after leaving the hairdresser in the bridal suite this afternoon, my brown curls were frizzed all over. "I met your father when I was five, and I certainly remembered him."

"Because you went to school with him for years after that. Petey was older than I was and homeschooled," I say, before adding beneath my breath, "And I'm pretty sure he ate playdough and his own boogers."

"See! I knew you remembered him," Mom says. "He's a doctor now, a pediatrician! Well, nearly a pediatrician. He's doing his residency in Minneapolis, which isn't that far to drive for a date. Especially if you do something fun on a Saturday or Sunday afternoon. He's moving home to join his brother's practice after he finishes his residency next year."

"Mom, no, stop," I say, my cheeks heating. "I don't need you to set me up with a booger eater."

"Well, goodness, I'm sure he doesn't eat them anymore," she says. "And it's not like you were the perfect child. I remember one time I came outside to check on you in the sandbox, and you'd taken off your socks, filled them with sand, and were bonking poor Petey on the head with them."

"I was probably trying to stop him from eating his boogers," I say, earning a hiss from Mom and a swat on my wrist.

"Lower your voice," she says. "His parents are here. The whole family is close with Seven's mother. Apparently, they've been frequenting her establishment for decades."

Mom says the word "establishment" like she's talking about a crack house filled with feral, unwashed dogs, but that's not a surprise. She's come a long way in the months since Binx and Seven first got together, but it's hard to teach an old snob new tricks.

At least she's friendly with Seven and his mother, and she's taken a genuine liking to Sprout. She even made the flower girl dress Sprout's wearing and added extra fabric to the skirt so it would have the "twirliness" her new granddaughter requested.

My mother is, at her core, a good person.

Even if it's hard to remember that when she's being a bossy matchmaker who can't take a hint to save her life...

"I could reintroduce you," she adds. "I saw Petey talking to Barrett by the bar just a little while ago. I'm sure he'd love the chance to get reacquainted, and you look so nice tonight. Your hair's hardly frizzy at all."

The woman must think I don't have eyes. My hair is a frizzed disaster, and it's about to get worse as soon as I head out into the summer heat.

No way in heck am I sticking around the ballroom to be forced upon Petey. I'll wait until everyone's dancing and sneak back in later, once it's easier to disappear into the crowd.

"Maybe later," I say vaguely, already backing toward the balcony doors. "I have to check on something."

"Check on something?" Mom's brows pinch together. "Check on what?"

"A thing I promised Christian and another thing for Mel," I say, trusting that my siblings will back me up if Mom questions either of them. I smile and wave, promising, "Be right back!"

But I have no intention of "being right back."

As soon as I close the door to the balcony behind me, I hurry past the few other people hanging out in the steamy July air and down the staircase at the far side. In just a few minutes, I'm on the path leading to the boathouse by the lake, leaving the raucous sounds of the party behind.

Mom can say what she wants about Seven and his "wild and rowdy" relatives, but it's the McGuires that turn every social gathering into a sound pollution situation. There are just too many of us. Eight kids are a lot to begin with, but now there are spouses and grandchildren and friends of the spouses and pets and friends of the pets...

It's just...a lot.

Especially for a person who wants to be left alone to read in peace most of the time. It's one of the many reasons I love my new job as a remote data analyst, working with a social science department on the East Coast. Sure, Zoom meetings are the worst, but that's only two mornings a week. The rest of the time, I'm left blissfully alone to pour through data, write papers, and make graphs.

Ah...a graph, now there's a thing you can put your faith in.

Not like people. People are far too confusing and hard to read.

Which, sadly, means my own matchmaking days are probably behind me. I loved the rush of helping two people find love way more than I thought I would, but I'm not usually good at spotting a perfect match. I only knew about Binx and Seven because she's my sister and closest sibling.

Even with my other siblings, I often don't understand what's in their hearts.

Barrett, for example. I had no clue that he and Wren would be ever be anything more than friends and colleagues. Their romance took me completely by surprise. Same with Christian and Starling. To be honest, I thought they disliked each other right up until the moment Mom started having a coronary because some jerk had leaked their sex tape to the internet.

I shudder at the thought as I step onto the dock beside the boathouse.

I would die.

I would spontaneously combust from shame and my ashes would be blown away by the wind, never to be seen again.

But that's one of the many benefits of being a twenty-four-year-old virgin. I don't have to worry about my sex tape being leaked to the internet, revenge porn, or STDs. I also spend very little time fretting about my heart being broken or accidental pregnancy.

Basically, life as an ancient, nerdy virgin is a bowl of cherries—pun intended.

I couldn't be happier.

So, why does my heart twist in my chest as I lean against the dock railing and stare back at the historic hotel, where all my nearest and dearest are celebrating?

I'm not jealous, truly I'm not. I wouldn't want to get married right now. I'm not even ready for a steady boyfriend.

My remote job might go in-person in the next few months. If it does, I'll be moving to Boston, and scoring a twenty thousand dollar increase in my annual salary. The last thing I need is an emotional attachment in Bad Dog tying me down. I already have the emotional attachment of my family to deal with. I know they won't be happy to learn that I'm moving so far away, even if it is only to assist on a two-year research study.

So, no. No boyfriend or fiancée for me, but a kiss might be nice.

Or maybe, something more than a kiss...

I wouldn't want to put my perfect "no dicks anywhere near my lady flower" record at risk, but the way Seven was holding Binx as he guided her around the dance floor made me wonder what it feels like to be held like that...like the person holding you finds you irresistible.

"Wendy Ann McGuire? Is that you?" The deep voice rumbling from my left makes me jump half a foot in the air.

"What?" I gasp as I spin to watch a tall shadow emerge from the open boathouse door. "Wh-who are you?"

He chuckles, a pleasant, rolling sound that makes the hair stand up on my arms. "Aw, come on. You remember me," he says, grinning as he steps into the moonlight a few feet away. "You used to eat boogers in my backyard."

"I did no such thing," I protest, making the man laugh.

He chuckles again. "I was just teasing, McGuire. Everyone knows my little brother was the gross one."

My eyes widen. "Connor Sinclair?"

"The same," he says, a dimple popping in his right cheek.

My jaw drops as my gaze tracks up and down the tall, muscled person Connor Sinclair has become. From his tousled sandy blond hair to the shining tips of his fancy shoes, he looks...expensive. Expensive and polished and too handsome for his own good—all things I hate in a guy.

So why does my neck hair join my arm hair in prickling to life as he steps closer?

"Shouldn't you be at the wedding?" he asks, motioning toward my gauzy lilac bridesmaid's dress.

"I'm avoiding my mother," I murmur, trying—and failing—to rip my gaze away from his. I can't see what color his eyes are in the dim light, but they're dazzling, even partly in shadow. He looks like he has secrets, fun ones that would be delightful to discover. "And your brother."

His brows lift. "Petey? Is he showing his ass? Do I need to remind him how to treat a beautiful woman?"

I snort and am immediately mortified. I cover by stammering, "No, he's fine. It's my mother wanting to re-introduce me to your brother that I'm avoiding. I'm not interested in being set up right now."

He nods, his eyes sparkling again. "Oh, no, you don't want to be set up. Especially not with my brother."

I tilt my head to one side. "Why not? Don't you like your brother?"

"Don't you?" he challenges, avoiding the question.

I narrow my eyes. "I don't really remember him. Except that he ate gross things in the sandbox when we used to play together. Call me shallow, but that's not the kind of thing I can get past, even if it happened almost twenty years ago. He was several years older than I was at the time. He really should have known better."

He makes a considering sound. "I agree, and can't say that I blame you. And to answer your question, no, I don't really care for my brother. Which is a shame. I like the idea of a close, brotherly bond, but..."

"But?" I prompt, intrigued by his openness. In my family, such betrayal of a fellow McGuire to a stranger, if discovered, would be punished by the cold shoulder and years of side-eye.

He shrugs. "That's just not how it worked out for us."

"But my mother said he's joining your practice when he graduates."

Connor grunts. "That's what my mother keeps telling everyone. But that's going to be hard to do now that I've sold the practice and am leaving town on Monday." He flashes his dimple again as he adds in a faux whisper, "How pissed is she going to be when she finds out, do you think?"

I blink faster. "Wow. You're..."

"Crazy?" he supplies.

I shake my head. "Brave."

"Nah," he says, his grin dimming a watt or two. "If I were brave, I would have told her I was leaving. I just can't handle the drama right now. I've had my fill of that for the next thirty or forty years."

I furrow my brow sympathetically. "I understand. My mother and Binx had a big blow-up fight last fall. The tension only lasted a month or so, but it nearly gave me an ulcer. I can't handle conflict."

"I can handle it," he says, "just not if there's no chance of the conflict being resolved. My parents refuse to see that my brother isn't a good doctor. Even if they *could* see, I doubt it would change their minds. They've always gone out of their way to pander to Petey. But I can't play along anymore, not when the lives and well-being of my patients could be at risk." He exhales a soft laugh. "Sorry. Didn't mean to dump on you."

"No, it's fine," I say. "Feel free."

"I just don't have anyone else to talk to. I'm keeping the move top secret from everyone I know until I'm on my way out of town." He smiles before adding in a softer voice, "And you have kind eyes."

"Thanks," I say. "You, too."

His eyes *are* kind, but they're also...magnetic. They hold me in thrall as he braces his hand on the railing beside me and leans closer, whispering, "So, what do you think? Should we bail on this whole scene? I have a bottle of wine and some fantastic maple cookies at my place."

"I love maple cookies," I murmur, even as my thoughts race.

A bottle of wine and cookies...

And his body is now very close to mine...

His dazzling eyes more sparkly than ever...

Could this...

Is he...

"Are you asking me to have sex with you?" I blurt out with another snort I'm too shocked to be embarrassed about.

He laughs, a tad uncomfortably, I think. "Um, well, no. I thought we could enjoy the wine, cookies, and conversation, and...see where things lead. But if you're looking for that kind of evening, I wouldn't be opposed to it." He flashes another charming grin. "As I said, you're beautiful. Stunning, really."

I fight the urge to snort-giggle and fail. "Oh my God, sorry," I say, still laughing. "I just.. I can't... Wow, this is..."

He steps back, running a hand through his hair. "No, don't apologize, please. I deserve to be laughed at. That was cheesy as hell. I'm the one who should be sorry. I was in a relationship for so long, I've clearly forgotten how to flirt in a normal, not-weird way."

"No, you were normal," I say. "Well, I think you were, anyway. I've never had anyone ask me home for 'wine and cookies' before."

It's his turn to snort. "Yeah, right."

"Seriously," I insist. "I've never had anyone come on to me like that. Ever."

His eyes widen. "Are the guys in your orbit blind?"

"No, they see just fine." I shrug as I push my glasses up my nose. "They see that I'm a nerdy woman with five giant older brothers and two extremely tough older sisters. Not to mention all my cousins and uncles and my family's very protective pets. With those odds, no one around here wants to fork around and find out what happens if they try to take me home."

He nods slowly, seeming to roll all that over for a beat. "I can see that, I guess. But someone should have stepped up and taken a chance. I have a feeling you'd be worth it."

"Thanks," I say, my cheeks heating. The words might have sounded cheesy from someone else, but he seems so sincere, so kind.

Would it be so bad to go home with this man? To drink his wine and eat his cookies? To make out with his sexy face and...maybe see a penis for the first time in real life?

My heart develops a case of the hiccups at the mere thought of it, but still, I don't step away or start back toward the ballroom.

"I'd ask you out on a real date myself if I weren't leaving so soon," he says, his hands sliding into the pockets of his suit pants. "But I learned how rough long-distance relationships are the hard way, so..."

"Well, we um..." I trail off, my heart racing as my tongue slips out to wet my lips.

Am I really considering this?

Just mere minutes after thinking about how much I enjoy being a virgin?

But then, maybe I would enjoy being not-a-virgin just as much, if I got to lose it to a man like this. And as far as I'm concerned, the fact that he's going away is a feature, not a bug. It would eliminate all the stress from the encounter. Even if the nookie is awful, I'll only have to risk running into him around town for a couple of days. If necessary, I could hide out in my apartment and live on ramen noodles and scrambled eggs for that long.

It's an ideal scenario, and I've been a statistics nerd long enough to know that those are few and far between.

So, I gather my courage and blurt out, "We wouldn't have to have a relationship. We could just...have fun. Until you leave on Monday."

His brows shoot up. "Really?"

"Really," I assure him, ignoring the fact that my stomach has dropped to my feet and something hot and frantic is happening in my intestines. "Assuming we have chemistry, I mean. We should probably figure that out first."

His lips quirk up, as if he finds me amusing, and maybe a little dorky.

But that's okay, I *am* dorky. I'm also a woman who knows her own mind, and isn't afraid to trust my instincts, and my instincts are telling me, I should kiss this man.

Right now, even though I've never made the first move before in my entire life.

But there's a first time for everything, a fact I prove as I grip the lapels of his suit jacket, push up on tiptoe, and press my lips to his. At first, he's stiff, surprised, but a second later, his arm is around my waist, his hand is in my hair, and he's kissing me like I'm the star of the show.

I've never been the star.

I'm barely a supporting cast member. My family has done their best to banish me to the backstage area, determined to protect the baby of the family from all the big, scary things in life.

But suddenly, I don't want to be protected, I want to be...naked.

Naked and tangled up with this gorgeous man who smells like exotic leather and spice and touches me like he's had my body memorized for years. I've never felt so instantly comforted and electrified by anything in my entire life. He feels so safe, so familiar, and simultaneously like the wildest ride at the county fair, the one I had to wait to go on until my overprotective brothers left for the night.

By the time we come up for air, I'm on fire, sizzling all over in a way I've only read about in books up to this point.

"I think the chemistry is covered," he murmurs, looking as hungry as I feel.

"So covered," I agree, still breathless. "Meet you in the parking area in five minutes? I have to go tell my sister I'm leaving early."

He nods. "See you there. I'm the vintage Mustang. Pale yellow. You can't miss it."

I won't miss it, I promise myself as I hurry back toward the wedding.

I'm not going to chicken out. I'm going to seize the day—and the D—and by this time tomorrow, I'll have put a very big rite of passage in my rearview mirror.

After all, how hard can a one-night stand be?

People far less accomplished than I am do that sort of thing all the time.

Of course, I have no idea just how complicated things

are about to get. Or that even nice guys can turn your world upside down without even trying.

WHEN IT SIZZLES, Wendy Ann's story,
and the FINAL installment in
The McGuire Brothers saga releases this fall!
Pre-order here.
Keep reading for a sneak peek!

And subscribe to Lili's newsletter HERE **to make sure you never miss a sale or new release.**

Sneak Peek

Please enjoy this sneak peek of
WHEN IT SIZZLES!

Wendy Ann McGuire

*A woman about to step out of her
comfort zone with a sexy one-night stand
she didn't realize she was looking for until
a gorgeous man kissed her senseless...*

I'm going to do this.

I'm really going to do it.

I'm about to lose my virginity via one-night stand to a handsome pediatrician, who is an incredible kisser, seems as attracted to me as I am to him, and has called me beautiful *twice*.

Best of all? He's leaving town in three days,

ensuring I won't have to deal with any post-coital embarrassment if I prove to be as bad at sex as I'm anticipating I will be.

In general, my self-esteem is healthy, but I'm not a sporty girl. Anything involving cardiovascular activity, strength, or balance is out of my wheelhouse, and sex seems like a pretty physically demanding activity. I will probably need months, if not years, of practice in order to achieve anything resembling sexual fitness.

Heck, it took three months of yoga classes just to touch my toes, and my downward facing dog still looks like an arthritic goat.

But that's okay. Someday, when I meet the right guy —perhaps a nerdy, STEM enthusiast who loves gathering data and testing a hypothesis as much I do—he won't mind that my carnal side is a work in progress.

Or, more likely, I'll have this one, rite-of-passage night before reverting to a sexless existence for the rest of my life.

Honestly, it's not an upsetting thought.

I've had a few boyfriends and kissing is nice, but not as nice as having sole control of the television remote after dinner or a bathroom to myself. I also adore sleeping alone. After years of sharing a room with my sister growing up and various roommates in college—and briefly living with my parents after graduation— having an apartment to myself is heaven.

So really, I have nothing to lose!

Except my virginity...and potentially my peace of mind, if I'm not one hundred percent sure I'm protected from pregnancy and STDs. I've been on the pill since I was a teenager to help with cramps, but I'm not sure about condom protocols.

With that in mind, I corner my sister on the dance floor and shout in her ear, "Congratulations! Your wedding was beautiful, and I love you so much, but I have to go."

"What? Why?" Binx's brow furrows, but the happy smile remains on her face. She's been beaming since she walked down the aisle to Seven, and who can blame her? Her husband is gorgeous in the way of action movie stars and professional lumberjacks.

And he adores her, a fact he proves by wrapping her up in his arms from behind and kissing the top of her head as my unruly relatives shout for the band to play Come on Eileen. The McGuire family party favorite is way too loud to talk over, so I hurriedly explain, "I met a man, and I'm going home with him. He's nice, and I'm not worried about my safety, but I *am* worried about diseases. Is a condom still good after a couple of years? I have one in my purse, but it's been there for a while."

Binx's eyes go saucer-wide. Seven steps discreetly away, clearly not wanting to stick around for this kind of sister talk.

"Wow. Woah." Binx laughs. "That was *not* what I was expecting you to say, but go, girl." She lifts a hand for me to high five. "Get you some. It's about time you let that wild side out to play."

"I don't have a wild side," I say, ignoring her hand as I push my glasses up my nose. "This is a reasonable decision that was quickly, but carefully evaluated. And you didn't answer my question."

"Oh, right," Binx says, blinking as her hand drops back to her side. "No, I wouldn't trust a condom that old. You'd better stop by a gas station or something. Better safe than sorry."

Lips pressing into a firm line, I nod. "Absolutely. Okay, thanks so much." Hopefully, stopping for protection won't take the wind out of Connor's sails, but if it does, then this clearly wasn't meant to be. I'm not about to put my health at risk to maintain an air of spontaneity. "I've got this."

"You do," Binx says, frowning as she adds. "But if you change your mind at any point, that's okay, too. Make sure this jerk knows no means no, even if you're already half naked."

My cheeks flaming, I roll my eyes. "He's not that kind of guy. He's really nice. And gorgeous and an excellent kisser."

Thankfully, Binx's whoop of celebration is drowned out by the opening notes of Come on Eileen. Only the guests closest to us hear her holler, and they're soon distracted by McGuires bouncing up and down all around them, like Irish jumping beans.

I'm about to make a run for the door when Binx pulls me in for a hug and shouts into my ear, "You're a strong, beautiful, amazing woman, and I hope you have the time of your life."

I pull back with a grin, loving my big sis even more. But then, she's always been my biggest cheerleader. If I do end up moving to Boston, I'll miss her most of all.

"Here you go," Seven calls out over the music as he returns to Binx's side. He reaches out, taking my hand in both of his. He curls my fingers around something with sharp plastic edges and says, "These are brand new. Got them from a reliable source."

My eyes fly wider as I realize what I'm holding.

"Be safe." Seven winks. "And have fun."

"I think I will," I say, grinning like a crazy woman as I wave goodbye to them with my condom-free hand and dash for the door.

Up ahead, I spot my mother camped out by the champagne fountain next to Petey Sinclair and a blonde woman I'm pretty sure is his mother and quickly adjust course. I duck down, shielding my face with my purse as I weave my way through the crowded dance floor toward the exit on the opposite side.

Mom's been trying to set me up with Petey all night. But I'm not interested in the boy who used to eat his boogers in my sandbox and throw his wrestler figurines at my head when we were kids. I wasn't interested the first five times she suggested we'd make a "cute couple." After kissing his smoking hot big brother down by the boat dock, I'm even less inclined to do so much as shake Petey's hand. Connor sold his practice and is sneaking out of town on Monday without telling his family, all to avoid practicing medicine with his kid brother, leading me to assume that Petey is as insufferable now as he was as a kid.

Hearing Connor get all passionate about protecting his patients from someone he doesn't feel is ready to be a physician was unbearably hot. Is there anything sexier than a man devoted to excellence in his work? And to protecting the innocent?

No. No, there's not.

I'd want to get naked with him even if he weren't the most handsome man I've ever seen in real life.

But, lucky me, he is. From his shaggy blond hair to his magnetic eyes to those broad shoulders and strong arms that felt so perfect wrapped around me, Connor couldn't be more perfect if I'd conjured him with one of my sister-in-law Tessa's witchy spell books.

The thought puts a skip in my step as I scuttle around a group of bouncing kids who already know every word to our family's unofficial anthem and duck through the door onto the landing outside the ballroom. Seconds later, I'm down the stairs, through the hotel lobby, and jogging out into the parking lot.

Jogging. I'm actually moving faster than a breezy walking pace of my own free will.

Connor Sinclair is already doing strange things to me.

Things I can't wait to explore more back at his place...

As he pulls up in front of me in a vintage yellow Mustang convertible with the top down and a summer breeze ruffling his sandy blond hair, I again experience that strange sense of being in the starring role for the first time in my life. Me, Wendy Ann, hyper-protected baby of the McGuire clan, uber nerd, ancient virgin, and girl voted most likely to marry a robot of my own creation by my senior class—they were a cruel group of teenagers—is sliding into the passenger's seat of a sexy vehicle, next to an even sexier man.

"For a second there, I thought maybe you'd changed your mind," Connor says, his green eyes—they're green, even more perfect—bright in the lamplight from the hotel.

I shake my head. "No. Saying goodbye just took a little longer than I thought. Then I had to sneak around my mother. She had your brother locked down and was lying in wait for a matchmaking ambush."

He frowns. "I don't know what she's thinking. You're out of Petey's league. Way out."

I bite the inside of my cheek, fighting a smile. But in the end, I lose the battle as I ask, "Yeah? You think so?"

"I know so," he says, reaching out to take my hand. The feel of his warm fingers wrapping around mine is enough to make my heavy pulse sink lower, until it's thudding between my thighs, and I'm very aware of the seat vibrating beneath me. "I remember you. Even when you were a kid, you were one of the smartest people I'd ever met. And kind. The fact that you didn't kill Petey for throwing toys at you is proof of that."

I blush, but feel obligated to confess, "Thank you, but I did hit him once. I don't remember it, but my mother said she caught me slapping him with a sock full of sand."

Connor laughs. "Good for you. Maybe if he'd been slapped a few more times, he wouldn't have grown up to be such a lazy, entitled pain in my backside." He squeezes my hand. "But I'm done talking about my brother. I'd rather hear more about you. What are you doing with that big, sexy brain of yours these days?"

As I explain my work as a research assistant and data analyst for a study looking into the efficiency of cognitive behavioral therapy in children with OCD, he pulls out onto the narrow blacktop road. It's a nearly hour-long drive back to Bad Dog from this side of the lake. Binx and most of the wedding party are staying at the hotel tonight. I was supposed to sleep in the "kids" suite with Binx's stepdaughter, Sprout, and two of my teenaged cousins. But as much as I adore Sprout, I'm so glad to see the massive Victorian resort shrinking in the rearview mirror.

"Fascinating," Connor says, sounding truly fascinated. "I initially wanted to go into psychiatry. There's still so much to learn in that field. It's exciting."

"Agreed," I say. "Why did you decide on pediatrics, instead?"

"I took a semester off to volunteer with Doctors without Borders. We worked with a community in Ecuador, and I fell in love with the kids and families there. And I seemed to have a way with them, so…" He shrugs and flashes me a self-conscious smile. "Probably because I'm still a big kid myself. And because it felt so good to have that kind of connection. I was pretty lonely growing up. I never fit in with my family, but when I'm working with parents to help their little ones feel better, I do. Pediatrics felt like a perfect fit."

I nod, my chest aching as I study his profile, silhouetted against the dark woods zipping by. He's not just a pretty face. He's as pretty on the inside as he is on the outside.

Be still my thudding heart…

"I agree," I murmur, warning my heart not to get any ideas. This is just one night. One night to enjoy this amazing man before we go our separate ways. "I'm sorry you were lonely."

"Thanks," he says. "I bet you didn't have to worry about loneliness, not with a family the size of yours. Seemed like almost every seat at the ceremony had a McGuire in it. Seven only had what? One row of guests? Two?"

I laugh. "One and a half. Binx was so embarrassed."

"She shouldn't have been. It's great that you have such a big, happy family."

I nod. "It is, but it can still get lonely sometimes. Especially if you're...different. My older brother, Barrett, is nerdy like me, but he's so much older that we don't spend much time together. He's too busy with work and family to discuss the latest article on dark matter with his baby sister, and the rest of my family couldn't be less interested in things like that."

His brow furrows. "Why? Dark matter is fascinating. It makes up eighty-five percent of the matter in the universe, but we still have no idea what it really is. What's more fascinating than that?"

"Exactly," I say, my blood pumping faster as I shift to face him in in my seat. "An invisible force not even the most brilliant minds in the world can understand or explain is underpinning our entire universe, holding it up like scaffolding and we are completely in the dark about what it is or where it came from. How can you hear something like that and not want to investigate it until your brain explodes?"

He glances my way, heat in his expression that makes me keenly aware of the warm vibration of my seat again.

"Has anyone ever told you that your mind is incredibly sexy, Wendy Ann McGuire?"

I swallow and shake my head, shocked to feel my nipples tight and tingling beneath the bodice of my bridesmaid's dress. "No, they haven't."

"Well, it is," he says, in a rough voice that makes me believe him. "Incredibly sexy."

"I think yours is pretty nice, too," I murmur.

"Nice? Just nice?" He smiles, a wicked grin that makes me want to kiss him again.

Right now.

So, I do.

I lean across the console and press a kiss to his cheek.

His voice even huskier as he murmurs, "Your lips are so damned soft."

"And you're the most compelling man I've ever met," I whisper, kissing his jaw, then his neck, my nerve endings tingling. I've never been this bold, but it feels right... perfect, even.

He exhales a ragged breath. "Should I pull over?"

"Pull over?" I ask, running the tip of my tongue across his skin, humming in appreciation at the clean, but lightly salty taste of him. Even his skin is delicious.

"So, I can kiss you again properly," he says. "If not, you'll have to stop. I'm going to run off the road if you keep—" He breaks off with a soft curse as I swirl my tongue against the pulse in his throat. "No more of that, Wendy Ann. Not if you want to wait until we're behind closed doors."

I grin, feeling delightfully wicked. "You wouldn't," I whisper, brushing the tip of my nose back and forth across his jaw. "You're a respectable physician, not a man who does salacious things to a woman on the side of the road."

"I'm a respectable physician on his way out of town," he says, his hand curling around my thigh, making the pulse between my legs beat harder, deeper. "And I could find a nice dark place to park so we wouldn't be seen."

I bite my lip, easing back into my seat with a hint of regret. "All right, I'll be good."

As much as my body aches to have him closer, I don't want my first time to be in the backseat of a car.

"Please, don't be good," he says, his fingers tightening on my thigh. "Be as wicked as you want to be, just..." He flashes me a shaky smile. "Wait until we're back at my place? For our mutual well-being? I don't want to put your safety at risk."

I nod. "Same."

Speaking of safety...you should probably let him know it's your first time. That would be good information for him to have before he assumes you're going to know exactly what to do.

Or before he rushes in, penis-blazing.

I wrinkle my nose at the inner voice.

Penis-blazing? What is wrong with me?

Penises don't blaze and my body was literally made to do what we're about to do. Having sex isn't like running a marathon, for goodness sakes. I don't need to train or ease into this with some kind of couch to 5K program.

I just need to relax and let nature take its course.

And to keep my mouth shut and refrain from giving Connor any reason to change his mind about our steamy night together. He's a good man, the kind who might have qualms about "hitting and quitting it" with a virgin, and I really don't want tonight to end in a friendly goodbye.

I don't want to say goodbye to this man until tomorrow morning, after we've spent a steamy night together, one I already know I'm never going to forget.

WHEN IT SIZZLES releases this fall!
Pre-order here.

About the Author

Author of over fifty novels, *USA Today* Bestseller **Lili Valente** writes everything from steamy suspense to laugh-out-loud romantic comedies. A die-hard romantic, she can't resist a story where love wins big. Because love should always win. She lives in Vermont with her two big-hearted boy children and a dog named Pippa Jane.

Find Lili at...
www.lilivalente.com

Also by Lili Valente

The McGuire Brothers

Boss Without Benefits

Not Today Bossman

Boss Me Around

When It Pours (novella)

Kind of a Sexy Jerk

When it Shines (novella)

Kind of a Hot Mess

Kind of a Dirty Talker

Kind of a Bad Idea

When it Sizzles

Forbidden Billionaires

Take Me, I'm Yours

Make Me Yours

Pretending I'm Yours

The Virgin Playbook

Scored

Screwed

Seduced

Sparked

Scooped

Hot Royal Romance

The Playboy Prince

The Grumpy Prince

The Bossy Prince

Laugh-out-Loud Rocker Rom Coms

The Bangover

Bang Theory

Banging The Enemy

The Rock Star's Baby Bargain

The Bliss River Small Town Series

Falling for the Fling

Falling for the Ex

Falling for the Bad Boy

The Hunter Brothers

The Baby Maker

The Troublemaker

The Heartbreaker

The Panty Melter

Bad Motherpuckers Series

Hot as Puck

Sexy Motherpucker

Puck-Aholic

Puck me Baby

Pucked Up Love

Puck Buddies

Big O Dating Specialists
Romantic Comedies

Hot Revenge for Hire

Hot Knight for Hire

Hot Mess for Hire

Hot Ghosthunter for Hire

The Lonesome Point Series

(Sexy Cowboys)

Leather and Lace

Saddles and Sin

Diamonds and Dust

12 Dates of Christmas

Glitter and Grit

Sunny with a Chance of True Love

Chaps and Chance

Ropes and Revenge

8 Second Angel

The Good Love Series

(co-written with Lauren Blakely)

The V Card

Good with His Hands

Good to be Bad

Made in United States
Orlando, FL
13 November 2024

53873788R00153